THE DANCER

STEPS FROM THE DARK

Seán de Gallai

Do mo thuismitheoirí, Nellie agus Gerry mór.

Acknowledgements

Thanks to my first readers: Caitlin Ward, Michaela Dillon, Fiona Pfaff, Brenda Ní Chatháin, and Shauna Curran; to my editors: Will Mawhood and Robert Doran. Thanks also to Sarah Kettles for proofreading, Averill Buchanan for her expertise in self-publishing, and Jamie Romain for designing the cover and his creative support; and to Declan Jones for being so tolerant and helpful. Thanks to all the people who inspired me, K.L.M, the children who I've taught through the years for saying and doing the stupidest of things. A special thanks to Ashlene McFadden. Without her help the book probably wouldn't exist. Lastly, friends and family for their continued support.

Chapter 1

The night before, Grandpa had whispered in my ear. He said it was the perfect time for a vaca. Mom, Dad, Lucas and I would be going on a trip, and it would work out good because the exterminators could come. I didn't believe in the termites any more than I did in the fat, bearded Christmas guy. But whatever, I thought. And we couldn't say anything to Mom. Or Lucas. He was all mouth. It was gonna be a surprise. She hadn't been doing so good lately.

Earlier that day, Dad told me to pack an overnight bag for Lucas and me, that our ride would be coming that evening. He wouldn't answer my whys. But the way things worked out, it wasn't the surprise he and Grandpa were hoping for, seeing as the house caught fire just before we were due to leave.

Grandpa came in quietly and told me to wake Lucas. I was just about to do so when I heard Grandpa and Mom arguing in the kitchen. I threw my head around the corner.

"Not on my watch, you don't." That was all I could make out between the finger-pointing and slurring.

Mom flicked her cigarette in no particular direction as she spat cuss words while Dad tried to make right. Then a little orange flame appeared in a box of papers Dad had set on the counter to burn out back. In slow motion, I watched the flame get acquainted with the curtain tail, and I stood there, not able to say a word. Mom was screaming almighty in between throwing her head around and shaking Grandpa by the shoulders. Lucas emerged, wonder in his eyes, then started to cry. Grandpa caught sight of me and ushered me not so pleasantly out the back door toward a truck. A bear-sized, bearded guy leaned against the pickup. When he saw us coming, he opened the door and shut it quickly behind me.

"Get ready to drive," said Grandpa. "I'll be right back with Lucas."

I tried to catch my breath and started chewing on my last Juicy Fruit, which just about kept me from screaming. The guy told me he was my uncle. I got out to find Lucas but the bear dude just stretched out a tree-trunk arm and shook his head. Grandpa came back and said there was no point trying to get out again, that everything would be OK soon.

Old Buck, bear-man, whatever his name was, started up the engine.

I stretched my neck in between the headrests, gasping. "Where's Lucas? What about Lucas?" I asked.

The bear droned like an old tuba. "Don't worry. Lucas will be along any second now."

There was a bunch more yelling. Grandpa looked over his shoulder, and he said "Damn" just loudly enough that I could hear. I spun round like a nervous puppy and looked out the back window. I could just about make out Lucas's frame in the darkness, a small silhouette in the back seat as Mom drove off, gravel spitting. Dad chased after, shouting. So did Grandpa, but he came straight back.

There were some darker plumes of smoke now coming out the kitchen window. Our little rectangular home. Faded gray. A figure ran across the field from the neighboring house, a length of hosepipe around his shoulder. The frosty grass crackled under his feet. Dad filled a bucket from the outside faucet. My heart was going crazy. I had a feeling things weren't going to plan.

"Grandpa!" I yelled. Grandpa stopped talking and looked at me, then back to the bear-man.

"You want me to follow her?" the bear asked him.

He thought a moment. "No. Just take Alex. Call me when you're home." Grandpa's voice was grim.

"What?" I yelled. My breath was short and quick.

"You want me to wait till morning?" the bear asked.

"Call me. I'll be awake," said Grandpa.

"But, Grandpa, what about Lucas? What about Mom and Dad?"

I didn't want to think about the past few weeks. The past few months. My breath almost froze in front of my face. Maybe the words froze as soon as they left my mouth. Bear-man wound up the window with a screech. Grandpa stopped him halfway and gave me a sad, kind-eyed look. "Everything's gonna be just fine, kid." Then he ran. I knew that look. I remembered that look. When

Star came back lame after our gallop. Just before they put her down. How could I forget?

"Jesus! What y'all thinkin'? We can't leave now!"

Bear-man's strong eyes regarded me in the rearview mirror. A final whimper escaped. I turned to watch my little house fade into the distance. Was it over? Some of it was over, some only starting.

Cold night air crept into the truck and chilled the tears on my cheeks. I pulled a stinky old blanket over me. I couldn't bring myself to speak to him, not even to ask him to turn the heating on, ask where we were going. I knew if I opened my mouth tears would come. The bear-man just concentrated on the dirt road, which wound for miles before we hit the freeway.

The sky was empty, just black. My hand began to ache, and I found myself clasping my very first cuddly toy. Beauty had survived fourteen years without a single stitch. I held him to my chest and sat facing backwards, looking for a star, a glimmer of light in the night sky. The taste of salt had replaced the taste of candy as I blinked repeatedly.

That's how I remained for hours, just me and the darkness. Perhaps it was the dull drone of the engine, but whatever the reason, exhaustion won over. I must have slept.

When we arrived at the house, it was close to 6 a.m. Old Buck, or whatever his name was, opened my door, and I snapped awake like an angry tigress baring her teeth. Even though his eyes were kind, I slapped his outstretched hand. I didn't want to get out. Why did bad have to happen?

4

I tripped over a toolbox as I got out of the truck onto the cold, hard ground. I swore at the night.

"Hey, kiddo, we reserve that kind of language for weekends 'round here, OK?"

"What about Lucas, Mom and Dad?" I spat.

"Like Grandpa said, they'll be along in a day or two. Now come on in," he said with a shiver. "The kitchen's warm, and Tammy's got tomato soup."

He may have been smiling, but it was impossible to tell because of all the hair on his face. I followed unwillingly.

The house smelled weird, like a candle store or something. My eyes struggled to adjust to the brightness. I sat at an old wooden table, and he set a bowl of lukewarm gunk and a stick of bread in front of me. I felt sick. A woman brushed my arm as I sat. I couldn't take my eyes off the bowl of red. It was a strange time for supper.

"How are you feeling, Alexandra? Can I get you anything?" Her voice was soft and dumb.

"It's Alex. Only cops and teachers call me Alexandra."

"Let me get you something to drink, honey," she said. Her husband passed her at the door, and they whispered. I strained my ears.

"Buck? Where's Lucas?" she asked, all concerned.

"Not now—it's not good. We'll talk later." He went back outside.

I must have been suffering from sleep deprivation. This woman Tammy was Mom, but not Mom. She was her older sister, although I hadn't seen her since I was an embryo. She wasn't as pretty, but she had fewer lines on

5

her face. Her hair was different too—curlier, cut in a bob. It was insane. I felt like crying or screaming at how messed up things had become, but instead I focused on the spoon, turning it over in my hands.

She left an earthy-smelling mug of hot brown liquid by my side and stirred in some sugar and milk. The color changed from dark to golden. My nose scrunched as I took a sip. I was surprised at how good it tasted.

"Tea," said Tammy, "from the old country."

"Didn't know you were from India," I said.

The house was like a mansion. All the furniture actually came from a tree, no crappy linoleum in sight. My eyes shot to a dresser at the back wall. There were photos of Aunt Tammy, the bear-dude and two girls, one witch-like, and a runty one with scraggly black hair.

A shelf lined with garish trophies drew my eye, almost giving me an aneurism. These crappy ornaments were made from pretend metal, decorated with crazy holograms. Some of them were baby-giraffe big. They looked ridiculous. There was a slightly less offensive heart-shaped plaque covered with medals. I couldn't make out the portraits on the highest shelf, but I did spot a crystal vase and what looked like a weird pair of tap shoes stapled to a piece of wood.

The clinking of the spoon brought my attention back, liquid supper devoured. I didn't think I liked tomato soup. Tammy fetched sheets from the linen closet. The bearded one was back now, rocking in his chair by the stove. Old dudes like him surely smoked a pipe.

"Reckon you need a pipe, old-timer." My smile was insincere. His matched mine. He tapped his shirt pocket, highlighting the cylindrical bulge. I rolled my sleepy eyes. A cat meowed and brushed its back along my leg. I rested my head on the kitchen table, the wood cold on my face. The next gesture of feline friendliness was met with a little kick. A yelp followed. Cat would learn the hard way.

"There's a bed ready for you, Alexandra."

"It's OK, pops. Seems this was all just a really bad idea. I'm just gonna wait up till you're ready to drive me the hell outta here."

He shrugged and rested his eyes. I wondered about calling home or calling Vinnie, but when I checked and saw it was neither night nor morning, I figured I'd better wait. My eyes flickered. He was right. Tomorrow would come quicker if I slept.

I tried hard not to think about stuff, and it was easy; I had become good at it. All I needed was a good night's rest, and I could figure things out in the morning. We all could—me and Dad, Mom and Lucas. Grandpa would lend a hand.

The logs crackled as Christmas burned in the fire. I still had to get money from somewhere to buy Vinnie a present. I had such a good idea. He wanted to start up a band— me on guitar, him singing—but a harmonica sure would give us another dimension. Man, would he love it. His smile would likely make me laugh or cry. I was lucky he liked me back. I remembered Christmas Day. The snow had come hard. I spent the day at Vinnie's with him and his mom. We just hung out by the fire and played cards, and his mom was so sweet she even let me have a couple of glasses of her white wine because it was Christmas and all. It felt like real Christmas. It was good to get away.

The cat brushed my leg again, but I didn't care. A clock ticked, or perhaps my heart.

Chapter 2

That night, the nightmares were intense. Growling dogs chased me until my lungs felt rinsed of air. They cornered me, growled low as blood dripped from their teeth.

I rode my old red Raleigh, my legs too long. I pedaled as hard as I could, a tsunami driving toward me as I made my way through the forest and across the Ohio River, through Cincinnati and beyond, and no matter what, there was no escaping. I pedaled with the deepest fear that I had forgotten something.

I opened my eyes and shot up quick, panting. The room was so bright, a brightness only heavy snow could reflect. How had that happened? There was a second twin bed opposite mine, the covers ruffled. I listened, half-expecting to hear Lucas playing at the end of the bed, but the house was silent. I badly needed to use the bathroom. My head began to swim as I stood, the cold wooden floorboards sending shockwaves up my spine.

I inched forward, holding the back of my head. I scrunched my eyes closed, hoping things would look different when I opened them again. They didn't. I had no idea where I was.

A door directly across from the bedroom had a wooden plaque with a picture of a potty. I rushed across, twisted the key and emptied my bladder with my eyes closed.

When I opened them and washed my hands, the girl in the mirror looked lifeless and fightless, her sallow skin as pale as the snow outside.

The blueberry mark on my cheek had a heartbeat of its own. It wasn't Dad's fault. My hair was sticky. I searched the cabinet and found an unopened toothbrush and brushed for an age. My teeth sparkled, but the awful taste that seeped from my stomach remained.

I scrubbed my face with scalding water, and for a moment, color returned. I opened the door, screamed and slammed it shut again. My heart tried to break free from my chest. I pressed my back up against the door, fearing it would try to enter, to get me. It looked just like the kind of ghosts in the movies—pale-skinned girl, white nightdress, doll in one hand, knife in the other, blood dripping. Was this a dream within a dream? I dug my nails into my cheeks to see. It was real. The pain was real.

I slid to the ground, struggling for breath as the ghost wailed and thrashed outside. An adult voice called out. I grabbed a plunger from behind the cistern and gripped it tight. It was quieter in the hall now, just a gentle sobbing and some hushing. A knock on the door startled me.

"Alexandra? Are you OK? C'mon out, everything's fine."

I gritted my teeth, but eventually began to breathe. I threw my weapon to the side and opened the door slowly. Tammy stood there, the frightened girl-ghost gripping her waist, face buried into the small of her back.

"I think you must have given Kate a fright," Tammy said. Wrinkles formed on my brow. I felt dumb for acting so jumpy. "Kate, dear, this is Alexandra. I told you we'd have a guest, remember? Didn't you see her in the other bed this morning?"

She shook her head no. My heart steadied. The child just looked back at Tammy in wonderment. Tammy nodded at her and then smiled at me. "Come, let's have some breakfast. I've made pancakes."

Pancakes? Big deal! I fixed pancakes for Lucas and me every day of the week. This place was trouble—old, bearded kidnappers, cats, spooky little ghouls. What next? I had to keep my guard up until Mom and Dad arrived.

The kitchen looked different as daylight seeped through the old wooden windows. Not even a hint of paint flaking from the frames. I pinched the bridge of my nose, waiting for the dawn chorus of sneezes, but they didn't come. The place gave me the creeps. Tammy's blender thankfully halted any interrogation attempts from the ghost-kid, her no-longer-scared face full of awe.

Before long, a shoulder-high stack of pancakes sat in front of me. I concentrated on the yummy tastes and tried to ignore my thoughts. I reached for the coffee pot, and despite a disproving glance from Tammy, helped myself. She was stuffy—a crummy version of Mom.

Kate sat opposite. Her patience finally cracked when Tammy took a basket of laundry to the basement. "Did your mom and dad die? Why are you at my house? Did the stork bring you instead of the baby?"

I spluttered coffee. My mouth opened to release some choice cuss words, but then Old Buck appeared with a bag of coal.

"Kate, I need you outta those PJs immediately. You know the rules."

His voice matched his huge appearance, deep but soulful. Kate gave me a gap-toothed smile. I grimaced. She might just be lucky enough to meet the tooth fairy if she wasn't careful.

Tammy eyed me as I set my plate and mug by the sink. Her mouth half-opened and then closed again. I had to take the initiative even though I was afraid to ask. Old Buck came to wash his hands. What was better, knowing or not knowing?

"When will they be here?"

He dried his hands and folded the towel neatly.

"Mom and Dad. What time are they leaving Kentucky?"

His face was motionless except for his eyes. Tammy took a drink and looked out the window. It took him so long to respond, I thought maybe he was slightly brain-dead.

"Well? What time?"

"Alexandra, dear, it looks like it's going to be a day or two before the rest of the guys get here."

Not knowing.

"What do you mean?"

Finally, Tammy perked up.

"I talked with your mom this morning. Your dad's car, you know how it's always breaking down? Well, it didn't start this morning, and it just needs a small fixing. They reckon it should be good to go by tomorrow." She finished with a smile. I eyed her for a bit, but didn't push it.

I found myself playing with the ring on my middle finger, a metal ladybug ring, so old the red was almost faded away. Mom gave it to me on my sixth birthday. I used to wear it on a chain round my neck, but it fitted my middle finger now. It was the ring Dad proposed with. When Mom lost her wedding ring, she got her finger tattooed instead. A tattoo of red and green roses intertwined. She said she'd never lose it. My eyes started to burn, and I wasn't sure why.

"You must be pretty tired, honey, from the long trip. Why don't you go rest by the TV?"

Like I had just had life-saving surgery or something. I scowled, but didn't argue.

The living room was enormous, which just highlighted the absence of Christmas decorations. It had a great big tan sofa that had recliners either end. They even had a piano. I knew how to play two songs: "Frère Jacques" and "Heart and Soul" from the movie *Big*. Dad and I used to watch that movie over and over.

I lay on the sofa, shivering. When I turned onto my side, a bulge in my pocket stuck into my thigh. It was Lucas's inhaler. I had a mini freak-out, thinking how forgetful Mom was and how scared Lucas could get. My eyes started to well up as I thought about everyone at home, wondering what had happened with the kitchen fire. It was my first time away from my family, and it felt so stupid to be sad. I told myself to get a grip; it was only for a day or two. I had to stop the tears.

I flicked the remote control, and cartoon animals pranced around the giant plasma TV. My head hurt. I pressed a cushion into my face and just listened to the frantic chase music.

It took so much energy to stop horrible thoughts drifting in. The harder I tried, the worse it got. More and more thoughts came, doubling and redoubling the pain. Somehow, eventually, my brain formed cartoon images at the back of my eyes to accompany the sounds of the television. I relaxed.

The place was homely, and the only thing preventing me from slumber was Lucas.

Soon I felt a chilling presence nearby, an evil, whistle-nosed she-devil come to suck my slight contentment away. I threw the cushion over my head at the door. She yelped like the cat. I sat up and tried to get my eyebrows to touch my nose, but the kid was oblivious to hints. She crept in, dressed up in crazy gear.

First she sat on the chair opposite, then she dribbled across to the end of the long couch. I sat up, hugging my legs to my chest, and sighed. Once she realized I might not bite, she inched closer and closer until her leg was almost touching mine.

"OK, let's get this over with so you can leave me alone."

She just sat there in front of me with a frig
lips sewn together, eyes curious, a crater of
her left cheek. She closed one eye and slowl
mouth.

"Did you run away? Do you like dolls? Have you ever played Cracks on Jacks?"

"Please?" She obviously wasn't the brightest kid on the planet. Didn't make me feel any better toward her though. "No, I haven't run away. What in the heck is Crackjacks? And dolls are for babies. Is that it? Are you done? You can go now. Your next batch of questions is at sundown."

She followed the whites of her eyes into a standing position. Her mouth hinged open, another question bursting for freedom. I had a closer look at her get-up. I didn't quite understand. You could practically see ice forming in the sky outside, but she wore tiny pink shorts over black tights. The shorts said "Practice to Perfection" in pink glitter. On top, she wore a black zip-up with some writing I couldn't understand. Funniest of all were the bright-white pimpled knee socks and blue and gold sneakers that were missing a huge chunk on the sole. She looked like a clown-kid gone wrong. I snorted and quickly wiped the clear-colored slime onto my sleeve. Darn cat. She giggled and bit her hand to stop.

"OK, smart stuff," I said, half-angry, half-amused, "my turn. What the heck are you wearing? How old are you? Where the heck is this place? And when's the next train outta here?" She opened her mouth. "And who owns the darn cat? I hate cats. Can we kill it?"

"Buttons? You can't mean Buttons. I love Buttons!" Her voice was like something straight out of a Disney movie, all high-pitched and cutesy. I felt like punching her in the gut.

"First off, child, you can't call a cat Buttons. Actually, first off, don't have cats — they are disgusting, vermin-eating, bird-catching monsters. Secondly, you give them a name like Cat, certainly not Buttons. You know cat poop can make babies blind, right? And thirdly, if you're gonna speak to me, can you mind the decibels?" I said, covering my ears.

She backed away toward the door. She made the same face I had made in the bathroom earlier. I changed my tack slightly. "I won't hurt the cat. I was only kidding."

She unscrunched her face, and a sort of smile emerged. My mouth painfully mirrored hers. "You can answer my questions or get the heck out of here," I said.

She obviously misunderstood my tone of voice, and she shuffled toward me. She tried to touch my face, and I brushed her hand away.

"What happened to your face?"

"Kick-boxing."

"You have pretty hair. I'm eight years old, almost nine. This place is called Lakewood, but downtown is called Cleveland. It's where we go to watch the Browns. Goooooo Browns!"

My mouth started opening real slow as I watched her do the cheer. Then she just wriggled her face and continued talking. "This here I'm wearing is my practice clothes. I do Irish dancing and I gotta practice because there's a *feis* in a few weeks and I only came tenth last time so I gotta practice because Mrs. Gallagher says practice makes perfect."

I frowned. I had more questions, but didn't care to ask. Her tiny face was perfectly proportioned. Her eyes continued to pierce mine, and my headache returned. They seemed to change color depending on how near or far she was from me. One minute they were ocean-blue, the next they were sea-green. I stretched myself out once more.

"What did you say your name was?"

"Kate."

"Well, Kate, shouldn't you be fixin' to go practice?"

She jumped and shuffled her feet, doing some crazy moves in front of me, her face serious.

"And turn off the TV before you go."

She did as she was told and closed the door quietly behind her.

I pressed another cushion into my face. My eyes began to water again, and I worked hard to block out the thoughts of how awful things had been, remember the good times or even just think of nothing. Thankfully, it wasn't long until sleep came.

Chapter 3

A bang followed by an anguished cry brought me back to life. I looked for something to defend myself with and proceeded to the kitchen with a plastic baseball bat in my hand. Darkness was setting in. I felt delirious.

I peeked around the kitchen door and ducked out of pure instinct as an object flew inches past my face and smashed into the wall behind. I froze.

"Who the hell are you? What are you doing in my house?" a low voice rasped. A girl about my age took a phone out of her pocket. "Don't you dare move. I'm calling the cops."

She slammed a cupboard door. Some cereal boxes were on the floor. She was a little shorter than me, curly red hair bunched into a beanie. I reckoned I could take her.

A can of beans lay wounded at my feet. "Jeez-uz!"

She stepped on a cereal box and edged closer. I could just about make out creepy green eyes in the half-light.

"Who the hell are you? What do you want?"

She grabbed another can and crept threateningly. This kitty was wild and belonged in some kind of delinquency resort. I held the fake bat over my shoulder, and as she came closer, I just kicked my leg straight up into the air as a warning.

She backed off, yielding the can with less conviction. Then all of a sudden, the fluorescent lights flickered, and Old Buck flashed into existence, a look so serious on his face it might have stopped the Earth spinning. We both just stared. Then he opened his mouth and started laughing. His face became lost in his sandy-colored beard.

"It's OK, Bailey, she's your cousin," he said through all the laughter.

The girl looked at me and then at Old Buck. She panted like a dog, dropped the can with a thud and raced past me down the hallway. My heart was beating so fast. I wanted to laugh with the old-timer, but couldn't. Finally, Old Buck straightened himself out, tugged his beard and set a basket of logs by the range. He was like a real-life ginger Santa Claus, except on Weight Watchers.

"That's our Bailey, by the way. Didn't get around to telling her we'd be having guests. She's all raccoon, always has been, always will be."

I smirked. Seemed it wasn't only me who was messed up.

The door slammed, and Kate entered panting, clothes tattooed to her skin. She filled her water bottle at the fridge and gulped. "Someone turn on the fans," she said, and wiped her brow. I looked outside at the freshly falling snow and shivered. She smiled and brushed by as I stood there not knowing which way to look or go.

I wished I was back home on my beanbag, listening to music, reading, chilling in my room with Vinnie or walking by the creek. The pond was probably still frozen solid; we would have been skating all day. I wondered, would Vinnie and I end up getting married? I pictured a warm summer's day down by the old roofless church. I'd get some nice candelabras to put next to where the ivy and moss grew on the stone. I'd wear a sleeveless white dress, and Lucas would carry the ring up the aisle.

My attention turned to the kitchen cabinet. There were some books behind the china plates and fancy cups. I needed something to help me pass the evening. Most of them were cookbooks, but there was a *Guinness Book of World Records*. With nothing else to do, I hauled it to the bedroom.

The world's largest collection of yoyos and the world's heaviest lemon were anything but entertainment. I had never spent this long away from home, and started to feel real antsy. My un-rest was soon disturbed when a shy Kate returned in her underwear, a towel wrapped around her head. She got dressed behind a wardrobe door. I couldn't help but sneak a peek at her skinny body. I was slim, but this girl was something else, all skin, bone and questions.

I pretended to read, and grimaced, but the inquest did not arrive. Maybe that's what I had to do with Lucas. Run him up and down Clover's Hill until he couldn't talk anymore. I flung the book to the ground and sighed.

The bedroom walls were covered with photos of Buttons and posters of cats and kittens, of these quack dancers she was so mad about. Everything looked so glossy and fabulous. There was a shelf above Kate's bed with more medals and trophies, and portraits of Kate in her dance costume, which was a green dress covered in orange and white vomit. She was standing beside Tammy and some other woman dressed in a tent.

"I take it you won all those crummy trophies? You practice to win that junk?"

Kate closed her eyes and made a face. "You know you don't win or do good in life without practice. I'm going to try and win the Nationals someday, and maybe even go to the Worlds, and if I'm really good, I might get to tour with one of the big shows."

I snorted. Poor kid didn't know no better. "Yeah, good luck with that."

"And it's fun! Anyways, what would you know? You've never even seen me dance. I know all the Planxty Drury set dance even though I ain't supposed to, and I'm probably the only one in the class that knows it except for Martin and Lucy. And the slip jig I'm doing now is too easy for me, so Miss Gallagher says, and what would you know? You probably can't even do an over-two-three."

"OK, squeaks! What is this dumb dancing you keep talking about? Walk the planxty? Argh!" I made my best pirate impression. "Slip jig? Slip-on-your-butt jig."

Kate's face was serious. Even though she looked exhausted, she did a few wobbly bits with her feet and threw her leg in the air, humming a beat. "That's the slip jig, or part of it." She gulped for air and panted the words into my face. I locked my eyes on her forehead and performed three turns of a pirouette ending with my arms out wide. Kate, for once, had no words.

"That, my dear, is dancing. What you've done is confirm what I had already feared. It looks dumb, sounds dumb and seems easy, if you're already dumb. Jumping around like a maniac is not dancing. There's no grace. No art. People who dance like that should be strapped into a chair. And supervised."

Then an image flashed to mind. Grandma used to fool around from time to time dancing like that. I was real young. She used to sing old songs too, real slow and sad, the words in Irish. She used to make me pretend to wind her up like a music box, and sometimes she would slow down, and then I'd know to wind her up some more so she could finish the song. So long ago. I was surprised I remembered. Poor Grandma.

"Nuh-uh, it's so not for maniacs. It's really cool. You should try it."

She didn't seem to grasp how much I thought it sucked. Her face was innocent. She just dumb-smiled at me. I tried again. "Is it for people who have no friends? Do all the people who have no friends get together and do this dumb dancing and then y'all get to have other loser friends?"

Kate's face reddened. "Nuh-uh. Not true. I do so have lots of friends, more than other kids because of dance class, and no, it ain't easy. You have to be real talented and work real hard. Just look!" She took the towel off her head; her shiny black hair fell onto her shoulders, all stuck together. She began jumping around the room, kicking her feet out, slicing through the air, inhaling while humming a tune at the same time. She danced like she was wearing a straight-jacket, her arms planted against her body, a short-circuiting robot with a toothy smile. I couldn't help but laugh out loud.

Kate stopped suddenly, pouted and jumped into bed, pulling the sheets over her head. My heart fluttered. Last week, I had been teasing Lucas. I took his slingshot. He chased me round the house trying to get it back, and I accidently snapped the band. My face got all warm. I thought I heard some sniffles.

"Hey, dummy," I said, "bet I can do that just as good, if not better?" The sheets became still. She was either dead or interested. "Did you hear me, little girl-ghost? Still alive? Oh well, I guess I'm the world champion dork dancer, now that you're dead."

A sound came out of her mouth, the beginning of a word, but she had stopped herself.

I continued. "It looked easy-peasy. Bet you I could do that no trouble at all. What did you say it was called? Dumb Irish jig? Karate moves with music?"

The sheet rose to life as Kate stood with a big grin. "OK, smarty-pants, we'll see about that!" She grabbed my arm and dragged me to the tiniest space between the twin beds, flicked her wet hair, retreated a step and pointed her right foot. She was suddenly a serious and determined teacher.

"Watch closely. I'll show you how it's done, then I'll break down the step. We'll practice the movements, and then we'll combine them all together, OK?" Her voice took on a new pitch.

I nodded, shocked.

"This is how we start. And five, six, seven, eight."

She stood to attention, some kind of preparation pose, like a Lego man with one leg pointed out front. Then she took off, galloping. She jumped forward onto her pointed leg and swapped her weight back and forth, all the while rhyming off gibberish words that must have been leprechaun-ese. I held my chin, nodding.

"Those are over-two-threes. Did you get it?" she asked.

"I reckon," I said sarcastically.

"OK, you try."

"Actually, just do the last part once more, where you kick your butt and hop forward. Please?"

She showed me a couple more times, but my mind wandered. When I was her age, maybe younger, I was so passionate about ballet. I watched ballet clips on YouTube and tried to copy the moves. But mainly it was horses. I wanted a horse so bad that finally Mom and Dad cracked. They must have saved up all winter and spring, but finally one day I woke up and Star was eating grass in the field out back. It wasn't even my birthday or nothing.

A click of fingers brought me back to my present-day hell.

"Alexandra, you weren't listening. You try."

"OK, ready, squirt? Here goes."

As if reading my mind, Kate handed me a hairband from around her wrist. I tied a quick pony and then repeated what she had shown me, but Kate shook her head.

"No, you need to pay attention."

She demonstrated the first part again, but I wasn't getting it right.

"Wait," said Kate. She turned away from me and did the first step. "Hold one leg out front, then jump onto it, kicking your butt and bringing this one forward."

I copied, and we continued until the three movements were done.

"That's a little better, but next time, kick your butt with your left leg when you jump," she said, although how she could tell without a mirror, I have no idea. She faced me and asked me to do it again. I was so confused. I jumped, landed and somehow always ended up on the wrong foot. I felt my face getting red.

"Almost! You're doing good, real good. Remember, whatever foot you kick your butt is the one that goes out front next."

She kept encouraging me, but the darn thing was like quantum algebra. She demonstrated one final time, and I watched her leap high and perform the simple moves with such needle-and-thread precision. I attempted to copy without thinking. But Kate burst out laughing, and I stopped in rage.

"OK, maybe that's enough for today. Not as easy as you thought, huh?"

I held my tongue and leapt into bed, pulling the sheets over my head. My turn to sulk.

"Don't worry, pretty Alexandra. Lesson two tomorrow."

"Go away!" I shouted. "And don't you dare call me Alexandra."

She giggled and left the bedroom, closing the door behind her.

I lay and caught my breath as my heart rate slowed. I was so frustrated, but at the same time, I felt more energized than I had in days. The dancing was lame, no question, but one thing was for sure: it had made me forget. For those five minutes, it had made me forget.

Chapter 4

I woke the following morning to the sound of crunching snow. I peeked out the window and saw some footprints in the perfect whiteness by the house next door. Then I lay back down. Kate snored quietly, stuffed bear asphyxiated by her side. After tossing for a while, I realized sleep was gone. Cabin fever. I needed fresh air. The evil mouse-clock read 6:45.

Old Buck had left his overcoat and hat on a kitchen chair. I closed the door gently, not caring how ridiculous I looked. Icicles formed under my nose, and my fingers burned even though I had only left the porch, the swing stuck rigid.

The house was number 47, and I needed to remember that because everything looked just the same, a house, a car, another car, a house, a yard, a get-me-the-heck-outta here. So different from where I came from, my little mountaintop house, handful of neighbors always willing to help out. I thought about all the neighbors here, twitching their curtains, cramming into your space. It was just awful. How could people live like this? There was no way Vinnie and I could break into any of these houses. I remembered a time when we were real little. There was this old house a couple of miles up the road, in among a bunch of trees. So we decided to explore it. We pried a wooden board off a downstairs window and crept in with our flashlights. It was so scary, but so exciting.

The place was pretty much empty, but Vinnie found a trap-door to the attic, which was full of treasures. Vinnie found an old map and a pirate hat. I found an old ballerina music box. It was lined with red fabric on the inside, with a mirror and a small, blonde ballerina who twirled as the music from *Swan Lake* played. It was the only thing that would stop Lucas from crying and help him sleep through the noise. The box didn't work right— the ballerina spun too quickly, the music played too slow—yet he listened to it over and over. The music still gave me shivers any time I heard it.

The sidewalks were clear, and I eased into a brisk walk. The snow on the road was old and dirty. As I neared the end of the block, I met a snowman, small and pathetic, wearing not only a hat and scarf, but also a jacket. I ran over and knocked it to the ground with two kicks. Dumb snowman! Christmas was long over. Soon winter would be too.

I must have walked a couple of miles. There were drugstores, coffee shops, fast-food joints and bars, all with stupid names like Paul Tone's and Little Diana's Dinah. Ugh!

I put my head down and kept walking until I came to the most incredible sight. It was the biggest pond I had ever seen. I didn't realize they lived right on Lake Erie. The wind blew waves across the water. You couldn't even see the other side, just the outline of a boat on the horizon. It was more like the ocean. It made me think. The world was so big. I wondered what would end up happening to me. Soon the chill really got into my bones. I turned back and tried to find my way home. I passed some more bars, a charity shop, some kind of art center and a bank.

My organs were slowly shutting down with the cold. The air I exhaled was almost freezing a few inches from my face. Burying my hands deeper into the bear-sized coat pockets, I found a handkerchief and a five-dollar bill. Smiling in this weather was painful.

A girl with long black bangs, no more than eighteen, swept snow from the doorstep of a coffee shop. She turned the sign on the door to "open". There was nobody around. She smiled, and I stopped.

"You open?" I cringed. Duh.

"Yes, we sure are. Come on in. Looks like you've been through the worst of it," she said with a scrunched face. Little did she know.

The coffee shop was awesome, more like a secondhand bookstore. It smelled of coffee, vanilla and intelligence. My eyes danced at the sight of all the books. Down back, they had a record player and a whole bunch of vinyls. I wasn't sure if they were for sale or if the place became a music joint at night. Grandpa had lots of records, stuff like The Beatles and The Rolling Stones, even older stuff like B. B. King. I used to love listening to them when we went to visit.

I was the first customer. I could have sat on a comfortable sofa by the window, but I chose an old leather beanbag down back and took my jacket off. The girl was straight over with a menu.

"I'll just have a coffee, thanks," I said before she extended the menu. She swiveled back toward the counter, glancing with a giggle. The sound of rasping water filled the room, and I rose to scan through the bookshelves. I settled with a favorite of mine, *The Catcher in the Rye*.

Soon I was sipping my coffee and reading, and energy flowed through me as the words fed my mind.

"Excuse me, thought you might like this," said the girl. She placed a chocolate muffin on the table by my side.

"Oh, no, I don't have enough money."

"It's on the house." She smiled.

It was double chip with gooey chocolate sauce, still warm. Delicious! Later, when I paid, I placed all the change in her tip mug. What the heck, right? Old Buck woulda done the same, I figured.

I was closer to home than I had expected, making a left at Oldfield and Woods, walking twelve houses down to number 47. It was cool to have such a great coffee shop so near, not that I'd need to visit it again.

Tammy was waiting for me in her nightgown at the door, anxiety scribbled all over her face. Old Buck was tying his big old boots by the porch.

"Alexandra, I was worried sick. You know you shouldn't—"

"Relax, Tammy, I was just getting some air."

"Yes, but you could have—"

Old Buck placed a hand on her shoulder. She stopped jabbering.

"Looks good on you," he said. I blushed and unzipped the jacket quickly.

Seeing Tammy's worried face both angered and saddened me.

"Hey, you mind if I call home? I have to tell Mom to bring the charger for my phone."

She looked at the beard and he at her.

"Um, is your phone an Android?" I nodded. "My phone is Android too; you can probably use my charger?"

I stalled a moment and nodded once before continued toward the phone, talking over my shoulder. "I'm gonna call her anyway, see what time they're leaving. I'll pay you back."

I picked up the receiver and wondered if I'd need a code for Kentucky. I had only started tapping the buttons when Old Buck gently took the phone from my hand. My head began to swirl. Tammy put her arm around my shoulder and led me toward the table.

"What's going on?" I asked quietly. My head began to swirl.

"It's nothing major. Let's just sit, and I'll explain everything."

The two grown-ups looked at each other and then at me. Tammy pulled out a chair, and I sat. The old man stoked the furnace.

"I spoke with your grandpa last night."

"And what?" Her face was blank. "They are coming tomorrow, right?"

Tammy didn't answer, and I felt the blood drain from my face. Hers was poker.

"We're not sure."

Her husband joined her at the far end of the table. "We both agreed that it will be good for you to stay here with us a little while," he said.

I felt listless, but my eyes flickered toward the talking beard.

"We have a good place here. It's comfortable, and it will do you good to be able to relax."

"Relax? What in the heck is that supposed to mean? I can relax at home. What about Lucas? And Dad? What's going on?"

"Everything's going to be OK, eventually."

I stood and banged the table so hard that my knuckles cracked. "What do you mean? Quit talking in riddles and tell me what's going on. I'm fourteen, for Christ's sake!"

Old Buck scratched his chin. "After I picked you up, well, you know, there was a small fire in the kitchen. Well, the fire got a little out of hand …"

"And?"

"Well, it caused some damage."

My eyes lit up.

"Nobody got hurt, but for the moment, your mom … well, you can't really stay in the house in its current condition."

I sank back into the chair, my head ablaze with confusion. "How much damage?"

Tammy looked away.

"Well, this I won't lie to you about, kid. Considerable damage."

Tears erupted. I shoved the sugar bowl, and it fell to the floor. It smashed, scattering tiny white granules everywhere. Then I buried my head in my arms. I felt Tammy's gentle touch on my neck.

"May as well get it all out," Old Buck continued.

I could feel Tammy shake her head.

"May as well, Tam. Sooner it's out, sooner it's processed and healed."

There was a short silence, and I looked up at the bear-man through a gap in my sleeve.

"Thing is, kid, looks like you're going to be here for a number of weeks, depending. We're gonna be lookin' at putting you in school during that time."

"School? Nuh-uh. No way," I said, slobbering.

"I'm afraid so," he said sadly.

"No way. No freaking way!" I roared straight into his face. "And what about Lucas? When is Lucas coming?"

"We're working on it. I'm sorry it has to be this way. But you seem like a smart girl. You'll make the most of it."

I pushed Tammy out of the way and ran, swinging open the kitchen door, startling both myself and Kate, who must have been eavesdropping. I didn't stop until I was under the duvet. Then I cried and cried. I thought about Lucas. Poor little Lucas who still needed training wheels. I remembered the day he was born. I was all disappointed 'cause I wanted a little sister, and Mom felt sad for me, although I don't know why. And she said, "Alex, you know you were supposed to be a boy, but it doesn't always work like that." And to make me feel better, she let me name the baby. And so I made a list. Five days later, my baby boy had a name. The tears came and came until I ran out of breath. I thought I'd never breathe again. The pillow felt nice and cool on my face. Finally, a little voice spoke.

"It'll be OK, Alex. I promise."

Chapter 5

With the last of my phone's battery, I Facebooked Vinnie and told him I wasn't coming back for a while. He freaked out and called—something he never did—and then it died. I couldn't even muster the words needed to ask Kate to fetch her mom's charger. The next few days just passed. I'm not sure how; they just did. I spent a lot of time in bed. When I did stir to use the bathroom, I felt groggy and nauseous. My stomach was lined with cold cups of sugary tea that I found on my nightstand. At one point, Kate came and grabbed a jump rope from the closet. She just stared at me, her face strangely devoid of questions. The door quietly opened and closed many times.

I dreamt I was on a fishing-boat, clinging on as waves the size of mountains beat hard. Swell after swell after swell. I dreamt of my little home burning to the ground, blistered faces, trapped in red-hot glass, flaming eyes, life exploding in plumes of red and black.

When I woke, I cried at the cold, white reality that was the four walls around me. All my possessions gone—my dumb dolls hidden in a box under the floorboards, pictures of me holding a newborn Lucas, Star, fishing with Dad. All gone. What remained to keep the memories alive? I felt empty.

Tammy came in, her husband behind her. I held her and cried until my cheeks burned. Old Buck brought me a cup of water and a small blue pill, told me it would help with my headache. I didn't ask questions; anything please. Tammy stayed with me and rocked me for a long time, her thin frame just like Mom's, yet with an odor of love, of safety. And then I lay numb.

When I next woke, it was 10 a.m., and strangely, I felt calm. My lower back ached when I rose. It was a Tuesday, I was told, and both Kate and Bailey had returned to school. Tammy had managed to enroll me in the same high school as Bailey. We were the same age, and I would continue my ninth-grade tuition, in all likelihood having to take the same classes as her. I was overjoyed at this prospect.

Because of how I'd left home, I didn't have a change of clothes, and my white vest, red shirt and torn jeans were beginning to ferment. Tammy took me to Target to get some new stuff. When she tried to help me pick out something, I just kind of barked a couple of times at her suggestions. In the end, she gave me thirty dollars and told me to take my time. She went to look at old lady clothes. Zonked, I mindlessly pushed hangers back and forth. I just bought socks and underwear no more than two for a dollar and had the checkout girl put them in a large bag. That left me with twenty-two bucks. Tammy was none the wiser.

At Kohl's, she bought me a pair of sneakers, shorts, pants and a pair of black shoes. Tammy handed over her card and signed as I stood by the exit. I guess I felt kind of bad.

That afternoon, I went for another walk. I decided to dress like Vinnie so that I wouldn't forget him. I remembered the charity store I had seen before and went to check it out. I picked up a couple of plaid shirts and plain black tees. I found a pair of jeans that fit just right and a pair of black pants. There was a cool emerald-colored sweatshirt, but I didn't have enough money left over. The dude at the checkout was really kind, though, and let me have it at a super discount. As he packed my items, I found myself staring at his hat. It was just a red beanie, but it had "E equals MC squared" written in blue letters. I guessed the colors clashed. Maybe that's why I kept staring, and as I left the store, the dude ran after me, his hair all sticking up. "Here, take it," he said. "It's clean, I promise!"

It was weird. Kindness.

That night, after dinner, I read some more of *The Catcher in the Rye*, but couldn't really concentrate. My belly was full of crawling worms. I persisted all the same.

Kate showered after dance practice. She placed a fresh tooth under her pillow before getting into bed. She looked so happy about it. I thought about introducing her to the idea of rhino hunting, but I realized that my sleep would be disrupted by the arrival of a tooth fairy later that night. She had been quiet for some time, and I knew it couldn't last.

"Alex, do you believe in the tooth fairy?"

I yawned and rolled over. "I'm not sure."

"Because a boy in my class, he said that there's no such thing as the tooth fairy or the Easter Bunny."

She didn't seem tired, and I wondered how to make her stop. "I'm not sure, Kate. I'm tired …"

"Well, this boy, his name is Marvin, and his dad is a ostratician or something, and —"

I felt like telling her the truth. "Get to the point!"

"Well, see, because if there's no tooth fairy, there's probably no Santa Claus, and if he's not real, that means maybe there's no God too."

I heard her shuffling across her bed. The light went out. Her teeth chattered as she crawled under the covers. I struggled for words.

"Good night, Kate."

It was dark, and I was tired, but I just lay there, shivering. Minnie's hands kept turning even though I had told myself to stop checking. My mind was aching. I flitted between total frustration and total exhaustion. It was hard that it wasn't Lucas snoring gently across from me. I had only been away from home one other time that I could remember, but that time was awesome. Dad had won some money at the track and treated us all to a day out at an amusement park in Louisville. We spent the night in a motel. I couldn't remember the room or being there too much because of how exhausted I had been from all the rides Dad and I had been on. Lucas was still too small even for the merry-go-round, so he and Mom just paddled in a baby pool all day. I must have lingered on that memory for an age, because next thing I knew, the clock read 4:20, and Tammy was knocking gently on the door. Kate got up and went about getting ready, but I just rolled right on over and fell back asleep.

Soon Tammy was by my side, whispering. "Things are better than this. You have to keep busy."

I stayed where I was. They couldn't make me. Tammy was back five minutes later calling my name, but I just moved closer to the cool, white wall. Not long after, my heart jumped as the duvet was torn off me, the cold air bringing out goose pimples. I leapt up, ready to slice Kate, and was shocked to see Old Buck standing there with a sparkle in his eyes.

"You're up now, Alex. See, that wasn't so bad," he said, and I shivered as I tried to make out the expression on his face.

The shower was free, and the hot water felt so good on my skin. I spent longer than usual at the mirror, checking out my new get-up, not entirely unsatisfied. The jeans were a good fit, but my left knee felt a little claustrophobic, so I grabbed scissors from the cabinet and cut a little hole. Soon they would look just like my old pair. Tammy stopped me in the hallway immediately after.

"Oh my gosh, what happened to your jeans?"

"Just got creative with scissors, Tam, that's all."

After drying my hair, I returned to the room and found a bottle of perfume with a pink ribbon on my pillow. I had no idea who it belonged to, and thought maybe the cat had left it there as a present. I sprayed some on my wrist and inhaled the sweet lavender and cinnamon. Then I gave my neck a rub before getting my sneakers on. Kate watched me from the door with an innocent grin. I tried to reciprocate, but found it hard, knowing deep down that nothing was better than anything. School would just make everything worse.

"Did you have braces?" she asked. "Mom said when I'm older I might have to get braces for my teeth if we have enough money."

"No," I whispered. "Why?"

"Because you have real pretty teeth. They are so white and straight. When you smile you look like the sun." She gave a ridiculous giggle. I didn't smile back.

"Alex, I think you might just be the prettiest girl I've ever seen. You're even prettier than the girls in the dance shows."

I felt a lump in my throat, hard like a rock. I clenched my teeth and swallowed.

* * *

Tammy took the girls to school on her way to her work. I took my time with breakfast. I didn't want to go to school and hated every minute as we drove there. Old Buck did nothing to make me feel better. I'm sure he saw from my expression how counter-productive I thought the whole thing was. He was too busy listening to analysis of a sports game that happened three days previously. Get over it, I thought. I remembered back to my first day of kindergarten. I had kicked up a riot, but eventually Dad got me down there. He had to physically hold me in my seat and bribe me with all sorts of candy. When the teacher came, Dad left, and I was after him like a rocket. Finally, we made a deal. He promised he would stay right outside until it was home time. He showed me where I could spot him from my upstairs classroom window. Class started, and I must have made fifty trips over and back to the window in the first half hour. After lunch, I went to check if he was still there. I guessed the principal figured he may as well lend a hand seeing as he was sticking around for me to finish. His shirt was off, and he was mowing the grass.

The school was real big and kind of highfalutin'. Everything was new, and the kids dressed like they were from a Benetton commercial. Old Buck and I battled through hundreds of students, moving like frenzied ants as the queen called roll. I struggled to catch my breath and get my bearings as we made our way to the principal's office. Next thing I knew, I was shaking Principal Dennaghy's hand. A regular hairpiece Joe-Suit. Old Buck spoke a few words with him, and before I had a chance to psyche myself up, Dennaghy was making polite with me as we moved toward the classrooms. I found myself nodding without listening, and I was distracted when I heard my name coming from behind a half-opened door. "We've got a new boy joining class today. His name is Alex," the sharp voice announced, before Mr. Dennaghy knocked gently and entered. I stayed in the hallway. He turned back and urged me to come in with a shake of his head.

The teacher was small and bald. His fat, mustached face went blank when I entered, and he fidgeted with his tie. Thirty or more pairs of eyes stared at me and howled in laughter. They stopped laughing pretty quick though. I just slinked behind the principal.

"Now class, this is Alexandra, a visitor to our school for this term."

The class teacher had recovered and shook my hand. I continued to suffer. He shuffled some books and papers at his desk, all the while scanning the room. "Erm, Alexandra, there's a spot down back, where Rachel sits." He made this weird face with his lips. "She's out … for the next few days. Why don't you sit there until we make a more permanent arrangement?"

Bailey's cat eyes tracked me as I found my spot and sat on the hard wooden chair. I cleared my throat gently. I glanced to my left, and a boy smiled. He handed me a pen and a sheet of paper. I blushed. I didn't even have a schoolbag.

The class was history. They were studying the Ottoman Empire. None of the words or names made any sense to me, which helped me relax. I just listened to monotonous facts and rested my brain and eyes, down back, out of sight. Turns out I rested a little too well. I woke myself with a little snore and snapped my head up, wondering where the heck I was. Everyone started laughing; the teacher just stared open-mouthed. I coughed and cleared my throat a few times, but my face burned like wildfire, and there was nowhere to hide.

The day could only get worse. I re-evaluated my plans for lunch. My best idea was to eat somewhere quiet like the library, where I could be alone. I just had to get through gym class first.

Ms. Baros reluctantly allowed me to step out from activities because I didn't have my gym clothes with me. I knew by the way she looked at me that she hated me already. She was as short as Kate, but looked some kind of body-builder. She informed me it was the last day for cheerleading try-outs. I told her I had no interest, but she said all the other girls had done it and that I at least had to try out. Again I said no thank you, but abstaining wasn't an option, apparently.

I stood in the middle of the hall with thirty kids cringing on my behalf. She handed me a pair of white pom-poms. I closed my eyes a moment and exhaled slowly, wanting to die. I read the logo on her tennis shirt.

"Gimme an M. Gimme an I. Gimme an L L. Gimme an E. Gimme an R. What have we got? Go Miller!" I did it at fifty percent.

She was completely unimpressed, and my face scorched. I dropped the pom-poms by my side. The boys laughed, and the girls whispered to one another, nauseous faces.

"Is that all you have? Come on, you can do better than that." One of the girls tried to mimic my accent. I clenched my teeth, feeling so, so angry and humiliated. I picked up one pom-pom this time. They loved watching me die.

"Gimme an O. Gimme an H. Gimme an I. Gimme an O. You guys know where you can go!"

One hundred percent. With bird.

"You are excused, ma'am. Another trick like that, and it will be the principal's office."

After a bit, I cornered the dorkiest, least athletic, glasses-wearing kid with acne and asked her where the canteen was. I was one of the first in line to buy a sandwich. I made my way to the library, and as my luck would have it, the darn place was closed. I found a bench a few feet away from the entrance, under a bare tree. Some kids goofed around with another guy's hat at the basketball court. I just sat in the freezing cold and unwrapped my sandwich.

Before I had finished my first bite, Bailey and two friends turned the corner, their arms linked as they strutted toward me. They made quite the trio — Bailey, flame-haired, a tall, sleek black girl and a short, pale, calculating type.

"Hey, girl, how's it goin'?" the black girl asked.

"Fair to Midland," I said, staring at my sandwich.

"You brought up in the Antarctic or something? What are you doing out here? Brrr! It's freezing!" she continued.

I took a bite of my sandwich and started counting the lines in the pavement. Then she said, "Smile!" and when I looked up she took a photo of me with her phone. I looked away quickly. She stood in front of me, inches from my face, hovering the way a wasp would. I worked really hard not to engage with her eyes, just tried to pretend she wasn't there.

"Well, get used to being left out in the cold, girl, you know what I'm saying, redneck?" she said.

I had mistaken her initial question as one of concern. How dumb of me. I continued chewing.

"Dumb-ass falls asleep in class. What about it? They send us the smartest girl they have down South," said the shorter girl.

I kept chewing. Bailey tugged them onwards. "Hope you choke on it," she said.

Two older boys walked by and smiled at me. They must have been in eleventh grade. One guy gave me a look that told me to forget about them. I looked down at my feet. My turkey sandwich smelled a bit weird, and I didn't really want it anymore. It turned out it didn't really want me either.

The final humiliating act of my first day began with my stomach making this funny noise five minutes before lunch ended. With speed and precision, my lower abdomen emitted lightning sharp pain that had me doubled over. The most horrendous vomit burned my esophagus shortly after. I tried to run inside, holding my breath, but was too disoriented by pain and the inevitable vomit.

With no idea where the nearest bathroom was, I just shoved by some kids and lurched to a trash can. Kids stopped and stared, mouths covered, and I didn't even care as I just spat the sick from my mouth and blew additional vomit out my nose. I looked up and saw the janitor's face, unimpressed. I didn't quite get everything into the bin. He stretched a mop toward me. The laughter echoed in my ears for the remainder of the day.

After school, I slept for a few hours before watching some TV. Kate came in dressed for practice.

"Wanna come jump rope with me?"

My stomach rumbled. I gave her one look that told her not to ask again. It didn't stop her from talking though.

"I've got a big feis in a few weeks, and I gotta practice my new steps 'cause I wanna make sure I have them right for State." There was a pause, and I kept my eyes fixed on the TV. "State Championships are in two months."

I smiled sarcastically at her real quick before lying down and closing my eyes. I think she got the message.

The house was quiet after dinner, and I was able to work out some stuff in my head and understand things better. I switched on the old desktop in the living room. It was password-protected, but it took only three guesses to unlock. I figured it might have been Kate who set it. I sent Vinnie a Facebook message telling him not to worry, did some research and then relaxed. I went to bed shortly after. Cleveland was a hellhole. If only I could set it on fire. But it was OK; I had a plan. I thought about the last time I had seen Vinnie late on New Year's Eve. I had sneaked out easy because Mom and Dad had friends over for a party. We met by the frozen pond and skated a while. I was going too fast, and as I skated toward him I couldn't stop. We both ended up crashing onto the ice. He banged his head pretty hard as he tried to break my fall. Of course, I just laughed at him. Then, still lying on the ice, he got up on his elbows and looked deep into my eyes. He kissed me softly, and for the first time, told me he loved me. I pulled him toward me, and we kissed under the twinkle of a million stars. It felt like heaven. could make the feeling come back anytime I wanted when I closed my eyes and remembered really hard. That night I slept awesome, knowing that the next day would be a better one.

Chapter 6

I found an Indians baseball cap at the back of Kate's closet and wore it to school the following day. News got 'round about the new girl's hurling incident, and it seemed like all the kids were lined up to have a go at me. So much for my disguise. The laughter, snorting and name-calling rattled around my brain. I never knew I could walk so fast.

Morning classes consisted of science, English and double math, and without wishing too hard, it was soon lunch time. When the bell rang, I headed for the main gates in no particular hurry, not wanting to draw attention. The kids seemed too hungry to poke fun. In the parking lot, I noticed the girl who had been all up in my face the day before. She was talking to a bunch of older boys who were standing around a beat-up red Honda. Two of the guys got into the car, and another long-haired kid sat on the hood, his jacket zipped to his chin. The girl kept poking him in the ribs, and he just kept laughing. She was not impressed. She glared at me as I walked toward them. I just stared at my feet.

"Here comes the yokel," she said.

"Are you coming or not, Vanessa? C'mon, quit being such a tease."

"Shut up, Brad. Get a car with heating that works."

Brad checked me out as I walked by.

"Hey you? New chick? Princess struts?"

I kept walking.

"Yo princess? Indians chick?"

I stopped and turned. "Please?"

Vanessa squinted.

"What about you? Wanna go for a ride? We're going to Neo's for pizza," said Brad.

Vanessa scowled and punched Brad's shoulder. He just laughed harder, his perfect teeth showing. I found myself smiling.

"Well I do have a hankerin' for some pizza," I said. This was awesome.

Vanessa mouthed some swear words to Brad and then flicked his nose before swooshing around and stomping away. Brad opened the door, and I squeezed in.

"So, new girl, do you have an actual name, or just like, you know, like being hollered at?" said Brad. His boys chuckled.

"Guess, depends what you're hollerin'." I smiled. "Is Vanessa your girlfriend?"

Brad snorted. "No way, dude. Me and Vanessa, that just wouldn't work." Once again, his boys laughed.

"Dude, come on! You say that about every girl you've ever dated. Brad's got commitment issues," the mop-haired kid beside me said.

"Shut up, Brian, you pussy."

And it went from there. We sat and joked and talked and shared a large pepperoni pizza.

I played nice with the three boys. I learned that Vanessa had only started in the school the previous autumn and was already making a name for herself. Her dad was some kind of big-shot who had his nose stuck in all manner of businesses. He was a big advocate of gun control, which had made him unpopular with a lot of people, but it was hard for folks to dislike him after he helped fund Lakewood's new football field. People love football. Football helped people forget how crappy their lives were.

Cleveland sure was different from home, but I guessed some things were the same everywhere. Brad was the alpha male, the football captain and a champion boxer—jock of all trades. The two other guys were just there to laugh at his wise cracks, although the kid, Brian, seemed less of an idiot. Shame he had such a boring name.

I told them that my mom had died working undercover for the government and that it was just me and Dad, that we moved around a lot, that he was on a research mission in the Antarctic, and I was just waiting for him to come back. I definitely had a future career as an actor. Brad was creeping me out. He kept staring straight into my eyes as if he was trying to see inside me. I made him pay for my food. As we left the restaurant, I just said goodbye and started walking.

"Where are you going?"

I smiled to myself and kept walking. "I gotta catch a bus into the city."

"You want a ride to the bus stop?"

I turned and gave my signature smile. "How about the Greyhound station?"

He paused and checked his watch before looking at the other two, who didn't seem so keen.

"What? You afraid you might get in trouble for being late?" I asked.

He looked me up and down again, and I just stood there, one leg kinda bent, smiling.

"OK, sure, I think I can do that."

Brad drove like an idiot on the way downtown, trying to impress me. He ran a red light and tried to get his crappy car to go as fast as it could. I didn't care. As I got out, I thanked him and told him that Vanessa seemed nice and he should try to hold on to her. His face just dropped. It was kind of funny.

Things were not so funny after that. I was worried that they would ask me at the counter to see Tammy's I.D. because I had used her credit card to pay for the ticket, but that was the least of my problems; I started fearing for my life. The bus station was dirty and full of creeps. A couple of homeless people lay outside the entrance, drinking beer. One guy plagued me for a cigarette and followed me inside. I rushed to the desk. Thankfully, the lady at the counter accepted my printout without hesitation. I had successfully jumped another hurdle.

My bus didn't leave for another three hours, but luckily, I had Kate's iPod, with its incredible collection of terrible pop music and Irish jig stuff. I sat in view of the security guard for safety, although how Old Joe would come to my aid if anything happened was up for debate, seeing as he was as stiff as a corpse and probably would be one before long. My bladder ached, but I just couldn't risk going to the bathroom. People at the station were like zombies, some talking to themselves, others drinking gallon-sized portions of cola, scratching their butts. It was more like an asylum.

Five or six people got on the Kentucky-bound coach, and thankfully, I had a seat to myself. I still really needed to use the bathroom, but a scruffy white guy sat opposite the on-board toilet, singing to himself. Another deterrent. But I couldn't sit and fight nature much longer, and just hoped the bus driver kept a close watch.

Everything was going fine until we stopped by the side of the road at an imaginary bus stop. An entire Amish family pulled up in their little horse-drawn buggies. It was an awesome sight, like going back in time, the dark carriages and clothing set against the snowy backdrop like something out of a horror movie. There were at least fifteen of them between adults and kids. If truth be told, some of the moms looked no older than me. One guy sat next to me, and I almost gagged at the smell—it was like he'd been sleeping in a vat of sour milk. He smiled at me, and his teeth, man, some of them were in Ohio and some in West Virginia. My stomach started feeling woozy. The bus driver turned on the radio, the chatter quietened down and the singing from the back stopped. Then I must have slept.

I woke as we stopped for another rest break. My heart told me we were almost back in Kentucky. I bolted straight up, feeling slightly weird, and realized I wasn't really breathing. I pulled air into my lungs. Mom's face jumped to mind, and she wasn't smiling. It was her angry face. My head began to swim, and I couldn't seem to get enough oxygen. The more I tried to calm myself, the worse things got. My heart hammered inside my chest, and I couldn't stop my head from twitching as my thoughts raced. I didn't know what was happening to me. I felt so scared, but at the same time embarrassed and self-conscious, wondering if everyone else noticed I was freaking out.

Everyone bar one lady who was on her cell got off the bus. I ran up the aisle, jumped off the bus and went around the side of the bus station. It was a moonlit night. Cold air rose from the ground. I tried to control my breathing, but my heart battered inside my rib cage trying to explode, to escape. It felt like I was choking, and I thought I was about to die.

I went behind a bush and urinated, air cooling the backs of my sweaty knees. I ran back on the bus, crawled over the Amish next to me and shut my eyes tight, counting to one hundred, hoping whatever was wrong would pass. Thinking logically just made me feel worse. I just couldn't breathe. I had to get off the bus. Something wasn't right. I grabbed my backpack and got off.

The bus driver joked with some coworkers as others risked the freezing cold to feed their nicotine habit. I pinched the bridge of my nose real hard until my eyes started to water, and I took a couple of short, sharp breaths and ruffled my hair. The layout of the bus station was almost identical to the one in Cleveland. A black man wearing a Greyhound cap sat at the ticket counter. I increased my speed, gulped some more and barged to the front of the queue.

"Please, sir, I need help. Please, quick, can you call security, a man just tried to take my purse," I said, gasping.

His face lacked alarm. He excused himself politely from assisting a lady who looked on in concern and pressed a little button under his desk.

"Please, I need help!"

"OK, take it easy, ma'am. It's going to be OK."

He unhooked the little gate and brought me through to the other side. A security guard emerged from a back room and ushered me over. The three of us stood close, and I tried to breath, but my head kept twitching uncontrollably.

"Ma'am, tell us what happened," the security guard said.

I started crying and couldn't stop, as much as I tried. Words came out between sobs. "A guy grabbed my arm and said, 'Give me your purse, please'. I think he had a knife."

The security guard took a breath. It felt like my tears were creating a puddle of water on the floor.

"He said, 'Give me your purse, please.'?"

"What?"

"You said the man said, 'Give me your purse. Please.'"

I stopped mid-sob and brushed my face with the back of my hand.

"Yes, well, no. He didn't say it polite like that. Reckon it was more like, 'Hey, bitch, give me your purse,'" I said, kind of shouting. It was harder to cry after that. The security guard sighed and took a notebook and pen out of his shirt pocket.

"When did this happen?"

"Just now."

"Where?"

"Outside."

"What did he look like?"

"I'm not too sure. It was pretty dark."

"Any idea, miss?"

I paused a second. "Reckon he was wearing a black-rimmed hat and black jacket and had a beard."

The security guard and teller both looked toward the bus gate and then at each other. The security guard mumbled and left. The teller led me into a back room, and I sat down. He handed me a disposable cup of water and told me to relax, which I did a little.

I sat there in the bright, blinking phosphorescent light for I don't know how long. My mind bubbled. I heard them announce a short delay to the Kentucky-bound bus.

A huge black cop came into the room shortly afterwards. He looked around, panting, found a chair and pulled up facing me. He had some trouble settling himself.

"Ma'am, we talked with some of the passengers that fitted your description and asked them some questions. Seems none of them know anything about the incident."

I counted the rows of tiles, one knee crossed over the other. I couldn't make it stop shaking.

"Now, we are gonna have to take each and every one of them in here so you can point out who you think it was, OK?" he asked with little enthusiasm. I nodded, but he waited. "OK?"

I nodded once again. Then he got up, real slow. My mind was still ticking. I didn't know I had come to a decision until the words came out. I stood up. "Officer, it doesn't matter. I'm OK. I think he might have run. I don't think he was one of the guys on the bus."

He exhaled and stared at the ground. He was wheezing, perhaps asthmatic. My neck and shoulders began to ease up immediately. I wasn't really sure why, but I started talking some more.

"Officer," I said again, with a little more authority. I stood up straight and tightened the grip on my backpack. "Officer, I'll level with ya. I've run away from home and, well, I don't feel so hot right now."

Saliva gathered at the edge of his mouth, but he swallowed just in time. He looked at his watch. I checked the clock on the wall. It was 11.30 p.m. He sighed. I sat down once more.

"Where you on the run from, miss?"

"Cleveland, Ohio."

He picked his walkie from his belt and went outside. Within an hour, I was in a police car driving back to Cleveland. By early morning, Old Buck collected me from the police station in Akron. I bypassed Tammy's facial summersaults and wordless mouth and went straight to bed in Kate's room, lay down and stared at Mickey and Minnie until my lights went out.

Chapter 7

The next few days came and went. Everything was out of my control, and I couldn't go home. Maybe I'd never go home. Maybe I'd never see my family again. Lucas. I was totally dry. There were dozens of Facebook messages on my phone from Vinnie asking me where I was and what was going on. The phone he had got me for Christmas. I couldn't reply. Tammy was seriously pissed. One night, when I got up to use the bathroom, I thought I heard Tammy and Buck arguing in their bedroom. Maybe I was dreaming. Tammy said to Old Buck that she wanted me out of the house, that I was nothing but trouble and she didn't want me around Kate. I don't know what Buck said, but Tammy wasn't pleased. Maybe I had imagined that. It seemed like I flitted in and out of reality. But I guessed Tammy didn't have any smiles for me, so it was probably true.

Kate looked at me weird and kept her distance. She had no more questions. I spent my time between the living room and bed. Sometimes it felt like the sun came up, the snow stayed gray, my eyes turned red and I'd find myself in bed, awake again, dark outside, the TV calling.

One day, Tammy gave me some medicine that made me sleepy even though I had only been up a couple hours. I went straight back to bed. I remembered Kate's alarm clock ringing and Tammy handing me clean clothes. I remembered her pouring milk on my cereal. She even gave me a cup of coffee. My brain only zoned in when I got out of the car at school. The principal walked me to science class. Some kids may have stared, laughed, pointed. Two boring kids invited me bowling after school. There were five or six of them going. I had no desire to go, but when my blurred mind thought about it, well, what the heck else did I have to do in my crappy life?

They were meeting at 6:30, and I went on down there. Tammy was visibly pleased I was getting out of her house. She even gave me ten bucks to pay for the lane. What those unforgettable kids failed to mention was that Vanessa and Dominique would also be there. The way they looked at me when I showed up … I didn't even say hello, just spun straight 'round and headed for 47.

"My, that was quick, Alex. Why are you back so soon?"

"The lane was gonna cost twenty bucks, Tam, so I just rocked on outta there."

Kids gave up trying with me after that. Even teachers left me alone. At least now I was getting maybe four hours of undisturbed sleep each night.

Thursday, my phone rang a bunch of times. A half-dozen were Vinnie. Reckon Grandpa called twice and some other Kentucky number once. I just couldn't bring myself to talk to anyone.

There were two movies on TV on Friday evening: *Predator*, which I'd watched with Dad many times, and a comedy called *Big Momma's House*, which I hadn't seen. Tammy, a little more cheerful, came and tickled my feet as I lay across the couch petting Buttons. She told me to get up, that I had to do something, but I told her I was exhausted, and she left. Ten minutes later, she came back with a strong cup of black coffee. It was two-parts coffee, one-part sugar. I drank it anyway, and started feeling a lot better shortly after.

She then suggested I get out. There were art classes on at the Beck Center and cheerleading try-outs someplace else. I hated all that crap. Back home, because I was good at gymnastics, I got asked to cheer for the school football team, but I only lasted one week. The girls were such bitches.

I stared at the television, but Tammy kept talking, becoming frustrated. I found it funny. She wasn't one bit happy that I tried to run away, yet now she would do anything to get me out of the house. Finally, I caught her eye and told her I was going to watch TV.

Shortly afterward, she told me that she had to bring Kate to Irish dance class and that I would have to come. It was a half-hour drive, and I wasn't allowed to stay home with just Bailey. Old Buck was moving some furniture in his truck for the woman next door. I said I would help him, but she just shook her head no. Hanging out with the bearded dude sounded a hell of a lot better than going to dumb Irish dance.

I was literally dragged to Tammy's minivan, and I soon lost my fight. Fresh snow had started falling, which looked magical in the darkening sky. I tried to catch a flake with my eye and follow it to its rest. We were heading to a place called Rocky River, which sounded cool. Skipping stones or skating was exactly what I needed. Driving through suburbia gave me a chance to hate this place even more, everything and everyone the same. Everyone smiled a lot, and I wondered why. How could they possibly be happy?

We passed a block of houses, a junction, more houses, a church, a school, a park, houses, endlessly the same. Women out running, men out running. I saw a dog with half a tail, just like Harper. The dogs were pulling their owners, people carrying around bags of frozen dog poop. I grinned. This was so different. Even though in reality, we were all slaves, here, they were robots.

We parked at a large two-story building with two separate entrances, one a "Traditional Irish Barbers". The sign was of a cartoon man grinning. He had a shamrock tattooed on his bicep, which he was flexing, and the word *Barber* was underneath. It looked like he was missing a tooth, but Tammy assured me that part of the sign had fallen off.

The dancehall was just a large room with a smaller room off the back. It smelled like fresh paint. The floor was wooden and dusty, with tables and chairs stacked around the sides. There were floor-to-ceiling mirrors at the back wall.

I was surprised to find myself smiling, unable get the image out of my mind—old Paddy next door, cutting bowl haircuts. The reprieve didn't last, as dozens of chattering kids piled into the hall, tugging at one another, running about. I turned to go back to the car, but Tammy grabbed my sleeve.

"Alexandra, wait. There might be kids your age here. Maybe you can make some friends. Maybe even take part in class?"

The expression on my face was clear. She released her grip, and I walked a few more steps before she called out again. "There's no point going out there."

The car was locked, and I kicked the wheel. Snow fell off the hood, and the alarm screeched. I leaned back against the minivan, fingers in my ears, until I saw a silhouette at the door pointing a key. The lot fell silent. Leaning back against car, I stared at old Paddy's barbers. I imagined a life for myself, thirty years down the line, cutting hair with old Paddy, married with fourteen kids and missing some of my teeth. Me and Paddy, partners in crime. I sighed. I would have cried, only it was too darn cold. I was out of options. I went back inside.

Tammy and some other parents drank tea and coffee in the back kitchenette, while a bunch of kids of all different ages stretched, skinny bodies having emerging from layers of clothing as though from chrysalises. There were more than twenty kids in total. There was only one boy, about eight or nine years old. He wore a red soccer shirt, a baseball cap and knee pads, like he had been skateboarding. He had a vicious smile on his face, like he didn't give a damn about anyone. I laughed into my hand as he ran around sliding on his butt, and I thought of my poor Lucas and wondered when he was coming. Then I felt sad.

I found a corner to crawl into and sulked, but soon became fascinated with how messed up the place was. The majority of kids were between four and twelve, but there were a couple of older girls, possibly sixteen or seventeen. A guy with a mustache arrived carrying the world's first stereo. An enormous lady followed, wheezing. They talked for a moment, and soon the fat lady, Big Edna, was surrounded by kids. Was she the teacher? Kate ran up and hugged her, as much as she could, at least. Big Edna pointed her tree trunks in a couple of directions and said a few words. Kate attempted the move as instructed. Again I laughed. I remembered when I first started out with ballet a few years ago. It was unheard of to do ballet in my town, and I guessed that was reflected in the numbers. It was just me and another girl and the teacher, Mrs. Rudzik, who was just so happy that anyone turned up. She wouldn't accept any money and just taught us in a back room at her house. She had a little old terrier that Lucas played with every time I went. He liked it there. So did I. I looked at the Irish dance teacher once more, grinning. Even though Mrs. Rudzik was older than the Earth and needed a cane, she was still a great teacher. My smirk disappeared. Maybe it was the same here.

Kate ran over to me, smiling like an over-active puppy. "Hey Alex, Alex, Alex?"

"What?"

"Alex? Alexandi?"

"What, I said. You had me the first time."

"I told Mrs. Gallagher about you and that I showed you how to do over two-threes. She said you can take part in the class if you like."

"Get outta town, Katie. Actually, why don't you hurry up and get the class over with so we can go home. It smells like pee in here."

Kate just grinned and jumped from one foot to the next a couple of times. She sure moved a lot. I totally understood why Tammy made her come; she was like an Irish setter that wouldn't calm down.

"C'mon, Alex, it will be fun. There are two more beginners here. And we'll be right next to you. Martin teaches the beginners for the first forty minutes."

"The first forty minutes?" I yelled. "There's going to be a second forty minutes?"

Kate laughed her baby laugh. "You're funny."

In my confusion, I looked around for another man, hoping I'd at least have some eye-candy to help pass the time. There weren't any other men in the room. The girls were busy fixing socks and tying laces, fussing over hair, stretching and doing lots of talking. The little boy zoomed toward us pretending to be an airplane. He slid on his knees, coming to a halt in front of us. I raised my eyebrows.

"Katie? You're kidding, right?"

Kate did a whole bunch of dance moves beside me, her face full of concentration. Then she stopped. "He's a really good explainer, way better than me," she said, grabbing her bag and sitting on the floor.

I buried my head in my hands and clenched my teeth, unsure of whether I wanted to laugh or die.

"OK, I really need to work on some heavy-shoe stuff because I think my hornpipe isn't as good as Nicole's and there's this one girl called Susie from Akron who's just amazing." She then produced the tiniest pair of black tap shoes from her dance bag.

"What the heck are they? Don't tell me you tap dance too."

"No, dummy, you dance in hard shoes so you can hear the rhythm from your feet as well as from the music."

I think my face was actually blank. "Oh, I just thought it was like ballet except with really awful jig music."

"Don't say that. It's not awful! And I told you before, you can't call it jig music. There are different types, and it depends on how many beats in a bar. They all have different rhythm, you know. Sheesh!" Her voice was all high-pitched. She smacked her forehead. "It's better you don't take it up, probably. I take it all back. You're way too dumb!"

I continued to smile, my feelings just a little hurt.

"OK then, short stack, let's see what kind of noise you can make." She tied her shoes and did some random little taps with her heels and toes. "Great! Exactly what we need. One hundred little girls with grenades on their feet. Where are the ear plugs?"

She stuck her tongue out and stood center.

"Hey, maybe you should count the time in your head and not with your lips," I said.

She just looked at me, confused. I watched her bang out her moves. She no longer looked like a sweet little girl, more like a determined warrior, telling the music when to rise and when to fall as she patrolled the floor calling the shots. I was kind of amazed. I guessed I didn't really know what Irish dancing looked like. She looked angry, or maybe focused. I recognized some of the moves I had seen her do at home, but many others were different. She stopped after a bit and shoved some stray hairs behind her ear. She gulped water from a bottle.

Mrs. Gallagher called a dozen or so girls over. They danced around like robots. It was like Chinese torture, the same thing going round and round. The music was annoying; I could completely understand why they wanted to beat the hell out of the floor. The only thing that confused me was why they didn't want to beat their heads instead. I tried and failed to make out what the instruments were. The stereo blared a bizarre arrangement of notes held together by a pulsating beat. It was nothing like ballet. But it did have something — like watching an ant colony go about their labor.

The class split into groups. The guy with the mustache was in charge of the stereo, and Big Edna shouted instructions. Some moms stood down back watching, giving their opinions; others nattered, uninterested. It seemed totally chaotic, but I guessed in there somewhere it made some kind of sense.

I watched the mechanical steps without wanting to. I almost felt sorry for these poor kids who were forced to dance like this. After ten minutes, the little kid with the soccer shirt ran over to me, sliding in his boots. He smiled at me and spiked his sweaty hair. "Hello, my name is Martin. What's your name?"

He extended his hand, and I stared.

"Missus Gallagher ask-ed me for you to learn some of the dances with me and Lauren and Debbie. Kate said you already know over two-threes. Do you want to?"

Poor kid could hardly speak English. He nodded toward two little girls who stood facing each other playing a hand-clap game. He kept smiling, waiting. I laughed quietly.

"I'll pass, thanks, kid."

"Are ya sure?" he asked, disappointed. His accent was unusual, lilty. He was obviously fresh off the ship from Ireland. "Ah, go on. Will you not just dance a wee bit? For a wee while?"

I smiled and shook my head, swept the hair out of my face.

"Well, if you won't dance, will you be my girlfriend?" He giggled hysterically and ran off. He was also missing a bunch of teeth. Must be an Irish thing, I thought. Soon he was back by my side.

My face creased with laughter as I stared at his tiny little head, his light brown hair sticking up at the back, freckles on his nose.

"C'mon and dance, will ya?" he asked, and stretched his hand to help me up.

I looked around, but no one had been paying attention, and a quick glance at the clock showed more than an hour of class remained. I closed my eyes and wobbled my head like jelly.

"Fine, whatever," I said, rising, towering above the charming Irish small fry. He led me to his dance corner.

"This is Blondie," he said, trying to introduce me to the two other girls.

"Alex is better," I suggested.

"We're working on our over-two-threes still, so if you stand next to me, I'll show you."

The girls moved to one side. Martin took my hand, his face totally serious. Even though I towered over him, I felt myself blush a little. I checked to see if we had an audience, but nobody was paying any attention apart from the two girls, their faces eager. Martin pointed his right foot and jumped, kicking his butt with his left just like Kate had shown me. I was surprised that I had remembered the general randomness of the move, and I mimicked him.

"Wow, you did it. That was good," said Martin. "You switched your leg every time. Debbie and Lauren, do it now, and Alex, you watch." He kept hold of my hand, and I let him. "Watch this now, Alex," he whispered.

The girls did the over-two-three again and again, moving from the top of the room to the bottom. He released my hand and asked me to do it three times in a row where I stood. He then asked the girls to do it again.

"See how they aren't keeping to the time? See how they take off like on a bicycle? That's 'cause they aren't keeping to the music. You know the timing already."

"What do you mean?"

"You hear the music. It's easy for you. Next time you do it, try to point your toes more and get higher in the air when you jump." He nodded in encouragement.

I was momentarily flabbergasted. I tried the moves, working my way toward the mirror, keeping an eye on my feet. Martin took a drink from his water bottle, not even paying attention, and I became really frustrated. The more I watched and tried to correct myself, the more confused I became. I huffed as I walked back to the three kids, my face blotchy with sweat.

"Not bad," Martin said.

"Not bad? That was terrible," I whined.

He took another sip of water and handed me the bottle.

"It's my fault," he said. "I'm tryin' to make you do too much too quick. Just never mind getting everything so straight, and try it again."

I didn't particularly want to, but I danced toward the mirror again and kept getting my feet mixed up. My hair started getting in my face, and I could see myself getting red and ugly. I hated looking at myself. On my way back toward Martin, I landed awkward and hurt my ankle. I grunted and sat on the ground nursing it, steam coming out of my ears, probably. The two girls kept practicing and listening to Martin's encouraging words. Finally, he came and sat by my side.

"Nobody is ever good the first time. Some people are never good, no matter how hard they try."

"Well, what's the point in even trying, then?" I asked a little too loudly.

"It's great craic, that's why. When I do it, I feel like a king. I love it," he said, and stood up smiling. Big Edna called him over. Some dancers left her group, and others joined. I went back to my corner to cool off. The music started, and I watched Kate practice her moves in one corner. Martin started dancing like a bunny juiced up on carrots. He zipped around, clicking his feet high in the air next to his face, thundering around, clapping the floor with his miniature tap shoes, a great goofy smile on his face. I was still in a bad mood, but I was intrigued by how the little man beat out his rhythms and vibes in a cold wooden shack in the middle of nowhere, in the middle of winter.

Chapter 8

School was school for the next while. Nobody bothered me much. Some kids tried to talk to me, but they soon realized I liked being left alone. Bailey was dating a boy called Josh from tenth grade who had hair like a girl. I had seen their two groups of friends hanging out together in the cafeteria and out on the football field. They poked and pinched and chased before, but now it was hand-holding, and it seemed like they were officially boyfriend and girlfriend.

Josh smiled and said hi to me as they passed in the corridor one day. He had these amazing dark eyes and a strong, angular jaw. That night, Bailey came into my room and told me to stay the hell out of her way. Like I had done anything wrong! She also told me she wished I had burned in the fire along with the house. It didn't stop him from smiling at me after that, either. I guessed he was just a little more careful about it.

Homework took up much of my time as I tried to catch up on Lakewood's way of doing things, and besides that, I didn't feel like doing anything but sitting on my bed, sometimes scribbling with a pencil or reading or checking Facebook on my phone. I still wasn't ready to deal with talking to anyone from home.

The living room became increasingly out of bounds, as Bailey had taken to spending her time there, doing homework in front of the fire, watching MTV. I couldn't stand being in the same room as her spiteful eyes. I didn't even know what her problem was. Sometimes I would listen to Kate's iPod even though the music made me want to puke. I had finished reading *The Catcher in the Rye* and needed to go back to the coffee shop or to the bookstore to get something new.

Kate's collection of books was appalling—fairy princess junk and kitty cat books. One of the books was a ten-year anniversary edition of some Irish dance show that was big on Broadway. I skipped over the performers' interviews, which were lame. The photos were pretty cool, though: long lines of Irish dancers kicking their legs in unison. I couldn't quite believe they could all have their legs in the same position, the same elevation, all at once. It had to have been a camera trick. It looked like synchronized swimming except with dancing. The photos made the show look atmospheric—the lighting and fake smoke and the live band to the side. All the girls wore dark, velvety dresses and were pretty and made up nice. All this was a million miles away from Kate's poodle socks and whack-job sneakers. They all had nice, lean bodies. Kate had a dancer's body, and I guessed I did too.

There seemed to be an equal number of men and women in the show, and going by Mrs. Gallagher's class, I wondered where they had unearthed these guys from. I could totally understand why a jock wouldn't want to be a dancer, so I guessed these guys must have come from some special colony, a remote region of Ireland where the sole purpose was breeding dancing males. Strangely, some of these guys were hot. I got really confused as I thought about the crazy little moves that Kate and Martin had danced. How did that mumbo jumbo end up looking anything like what was in the book?

Although it all looked very glamorous, I was still mostly unimpressed. It made me wish I had kept up my ballet classes. And that made me miss home.

That evening, I knocked on Tammy's bedroom door. She was in bed, reading. I sat on the edge of the bed, unable to speak. Tammy just stared at me and encouraged me with her eyes. Finally, I got the words out. "Tammy, I'm begging you. Can't you fix it for me to go home? What's happening with Lucas? What's happening with the house? I miss my family."

She pursed her lips. "Alex, if it was possible, we would. It's just not possible at the moment. I'm sorry."

"But Tammy, what about Lucas? I can't stay here." I felt my throat tighten. The words didn't want to come out, and tears were nearby. I concentrated on the rug by Tammy's bed. I twiddled my thumbs.

"Lucas, in all likelihood, won't be coming now. The plans have kind of changed."

"Why can't I just go and stay with Grandpa? Or with Vinnie and his Mom?"

"I can't really answer those questions right now. All I know is your parents, Grandpa and I decided on this. Trust me, Alex, we aren't keeping you here as a prisoner. It's just … It's just got to be like this for a little while longer. You'll be home before you know it. I promise."

* * *

On Wednesday evening, Tammy came into the bedroom as I was drawing big teeth and mustaches in one of Kate's Irish dance books.

"Hey, Alex, how are you?"

I looked at her with my eyebrows and continued decorating faces. "Fine."

"Oh, that's good. Boy, I'm so tired. And I just made dinner, and I have to go do laundry, and I have to go in to work later."

I was slowly starting to piece together what she was getting at, and the yell from Bailey's room earlier now made sense.

"You know, sometimes I wish you guys were old enough to drive."

I flung the pen at the magazine. "Out with it, Tammy."

"Will you help me with the grocery shopping?"

I rolled my eyes and jumped up, looking for my sneakers. "Ugh! Next time, just ask. Straight up ask, Tammy." I left, mumbling. "Wasting all our lives waitin' to get to the point. Sheesh!"

As Tammy packed the groceries, I read the notice board outside. There was an advertisement for ballet classes in The Beck Center for the Arts, every Tuesday and Thursday at seven. The first class was free. On the car ride home, I decided. The Beck Center was only a couple of blocks away. I knew I had to do something.

Kate came into the room all sweaty, and I guessed she had been dancing out in the garage. That would have explained the noise I heard coming from there. I packed some stuff into a backpack. She was panting, but cheery as ever.

"Boy, do I feel great!"

She sounded like a commercial for health products.

"Alex, how come you don't come and practice your steps with me sometime?"

"Because, child, Irish dancing is for dumb-bums and doodle-whoppers and I am neither of those things."

She looked up in alarm. "But does that make me a dumb-bum and doodle-whopper too?"

I couldn't help myself. "Yes. Yes it does."

When the crevice in her cheek began to disappear and her eyes started to widen as if she was about to cry, I gave her a quick smack on the butt. It sounded worse than it was, but it helped. Her mood changed, and I spoke quickly.

"Truth is, Katie, I don't have much time for Irish dancing. It looks like robots from outer space with zero creativity. Everyone smells like cabbage. And bottom line: I ain't very good at it."

Before she could complain, I hushed her with a finger. "But lil Kat, I have absolutely no problem if you like it or if you wanna be the best dumb-whopper that does it. You go be the best and get in one of those dance shows."

Her eyes lit up, and she bounced on my bed. I hated people touching my stuff.

"You know, what you say isn't true."

I exhaled through my nose and stared at the white wall. "It is for dummies, kid, but—"

"No, not that, you so are good at it. You're a real natural. I even heard Mrs. Gallagher say you had a wonderful gait or something."

"What the heck is a gait? Is she talking about my ass?" I asked, kind of annoyed.

Kate giggled into her hand, and I eventually cracked a smile.

"And Martin keeps asking where you are."

"Oh, Martin will be fine. He did just fine before he met me."

"He said you were a real-life princess and he was going to marry you!"

"Reckon Martin may be somewhat … special. He's Irish, right?"

Kate nodded.

"There's something wrong with the water over there, or else with the potatoes." I pulled a funny face with my teeth pointing out, and Kate laughed and fell off the bed. She sure was a pain in the butt.

* * *

During school, I thought about how I'd sneak out of the house for ballet. We normally ate dinner at six, but I made a big cheese and sausage omelet after school and told Tammy I'd have a late dinner. Then I checked on Kate. She was in the living room, watching some garbage TV that tried to depict real-life high school — the typical mixture of teen angst, love and the supernatural.

"Hey, Kate," I said calmly. "What's this you're watching?"

"*My Babysitter's a Vampire,*" she answered, eyes still fixed on the screen.

"Oh yeah? What's it about?"

She stared at me, and her mouth dropped open as she rolled her eyes.

"Are you going dancing later?"

Her stare intensified.

"OK, cool. Well, have fun. I'm feeling a little funky, so I'm just gonna lie down for the evening, OK?"

I sat on my bed, bloated from eating so much healthy garbage. There was another weird tingle in my tummy, one I hadn't had in a long time. It wasn't like I wanted to attract trouble, but this one was necessary.

The biggest problem was getting out the front door without having to give a lame-ass excuse. We weren't allowed out after dark unless it was for something specific.

Just before seven, I swallowed a lungful of air and tippy-toed out the room. The light was on in Tammy's bedroom, and luckily, Old Buck was snoring on the couch. Bailey was in her bedroom with Josh, and Kate was in the garage, dancing as per usual. Every crunching footstep reverberated in my eardrums and scared me half to death. Soon I was marching free on open pavement.

I was so nervous as I approached the red-lit Beck Center and then stood in line to register. I kept looking around, thinking somebody would jump out and catch me and haul me back to the house. The receptionist must have noticed, because she asked me if I was feeling OK. I took a deep breath and nodded.

It turned out the dance class was for adult beginners. There were fifteen of us at the open session. The ballet teacher was at least six foot, with lots of creases on her brow. She regarded me with her beady little eyes as I lined up alongside the older women. Her gaze rested on me for an uncomfortable moment. I knew she would hate me.

We started off at the barre. My body was so stiff, and it hurt like hell for the first while, but gradually my muscles loosened. We practiced pliés and demi-pliés. The teacher, Ms. Allen, had toured with several different companies, mainly around Europe, she told us.

She spent time with each and every student, bending elbows, encouraging everyone except me. As I pirouetted, she straightened my knee roughly and poked my chin. I staggered, almost falling, before correcting myself and blushing, both embarrassed and angry.

"You know, this is an adult class," she said crossly, her accent British but soft. She didn't blink once.

"I, I'm sorry … I didn't know."

"Plant your left leg firmly. See me after class."

She moved along to the next lady, leaving me with a sense of despair. I had been enjoying the lesson despite the teacher. My body open up, blood flowing through my muscles, my mind fixed on the task. But then I withered as thoughts of home and my family came to visit.

I pulled my bottoms on quickly after class and headed for the door, but a shout from Ms. Allen halted me.

"Excuse me, ma'am, just a second."

I turned. She ordered me back with a flick of her head. I stood by her side and waited as she said goodbye to the other women. Finally, she turned to me.

"I'm afraid you can't come back to this class next week."

My heart sank, and I bowed my head, nodding. Part of me wanted to call her every name under the sun. I knew she didn't like me because of the way she squinted at me, the way she corrected me. I could feel my eyes begin to water and headed quickly for the door, both sad and furious that nothing would ever work out for me.

"Wait. I wasn't finished."

I turned and glowered, wiping my eyes. She stood squinting at me once more, cleaned a pair of glasses on her shirt and put them on. Her eyes opened large.

"You have lots of talent, em?"

"Alexandra, Alex," I replied.

"Wonderful. You would be more suited to the intermediate class, which I hold on the same nights except from eight to nine-thirty."

I was shocked.

"The classes last for eight weeks and cost $60 for the term, or you can pay a drop-in fee of ten dollars per class." She smiled, and I smiled back. "So hopefully, I'll see you on Tuesday. You'll be ready for advanced in no time."

I thanked her, blushed and turned to leave, my head reeling, my heart jumping and pirouetting into the night sky as I bounded home. There was one nagging issue — the money. But I would figure it out. I wasn't going to let something trivial like money ruin the good feelings that swept me all the way home.

Chapter 9

On Saturday, Tammy and Old Buck decided to take us out for dinner. I guessed she didn't feel like cooking, and I was only really surprised because this was the first time we had eaten out, and Mom and Dad used to bring Lucas and me to the bar for food almost every weekend. I hated going out with Mom and Dad at weekends. It almost always ended bad. But I guessed Tammy wanted to get me out of the bedroom and Kate out of the garage. Old Buck had come home late every night covered in grease, as he was helping his friend fix up a car. He looked like a thirsty old bear.

The place was called O'Malley's, and it was better than it sounded. It was a great big restaurant, tables and booths all around the outside, plant boxes in all the corners, giant palm tree on the closed-off patio and a large square bar in the center. As soon as I walked in, the smell of buffalo wings smacked me right in the face. There were TV screens above the bar, where guys of all ages and sizes sat watching sports and drinking beer. Old Buck couldn't help but check the scores, and within two minutes, Tammy insisted they swap seats so as he could avoid "neck strain". Buck just glowered and guzzled beer.

I sat beside Kate and read the menu over and over just so I didn't have to look at Bailey's puss face opposite. She sat texting — Josh, presumably — her phone beeping every few minutes. Kate slurped her soda, inflated the paper in which the straw came and nibbled nachos. She sure was annoying, but at least she was quiet.

Old Buck downed his light beer and anxiously tried to catch the waiter's eye.

"You want something, Tam? Maybe a glass of wine?" She sipped her ice water and shook her head. "Come on. We've worked long and hard all week. We never get out anymore."

Her face melted a little as she regarded his big old smile. Finally, she nodded. "OK, I guess a Cabernet would be nice."

Soon the food arrived. Bailer-exia ordered some kind of goat cheese salad. The thought of cheese coming out of a goat made me want to vomit and completely put me off my wings. What next, I wondered. Donkey cheese? Old Buck asked me if I wanted some buffalo mozzarella to go along with my buffalo wings, and I almost had to walk away. He just chugged on his beer and gnawed his 12 oz. steak, just like I thought he would. Tammy had some kind of fish and a side salad. Kate had chicken tenders and fries. The wine quickly loosened up Tammy's tongue. She startled to babble more than Kate.

She talked about helping old Mr. Such-and-Such at the nursing home and how his son came to visit him every Tuesday and Saturday and would bring him out for a walk and about some old dear who had recently died. I felt like blowing bubbles in my soda.

"Oh, Alexandra, cheer up, honey," she said as soon as she was done pushing salad around her plate. Then she just kept staring at me. I folded my napkin into a random shape and hoped Kate would strike up a dumb conversation. Instead, she focused on coloring in her place mat—the kind normally reserved for bratty toddlers.

After a few seconds, I looked up, and Tammy was still staring. She had now grabbed Old Buck's hand and was squeezing the knuckles white. She had a funny smile on her face that reminded me of Mom more than ever. She focused her gaze on the distance, and the smile remained stapled in place.

"Isn't it funny how it works, life? Not so long ago we were trying to add to our family ..." The sentence trailed off. Something in my stomach told me to leave, but I just held my breath and hoped it was over.

"You are such a pretty girl, Alexandra."

The words came out slow. Her voice was way different from normal, and she really emphasized the word "such". Old Buck wiped his beard with his free hand. Tammy was still smiling, but I knew she was working hard. Her right eye was twitching.

"Just like your father. He was such a handsome man."

I wanted it to end so bad. Whatever it was that was going on with Tammy, it scared me, just like with Mom, but different. Kate's coloring hand slowed down. I grabbed a free crayon and started helping. Bailey stopped texting and just stared blankly at her phone.

"And I always wanted a little golden-haired daughter."

The tears were coming now, Bailey's smirk-face long gone. Buck took a sip of beer.

"And years, later, well, there you go …"

She leaned her head into Buck's shoulder and sobbed. My throat stung as I concentrated on the coloring. Kate just looked at her mother.

"Mom? Mom, what's the matter with you?"

"It's funny how it works," she mumbled through her tears.

Old Buck pushed his plate away, and it clinked into Bailey's. He handed her the car keys.

"Kids, get in the car. Your mom's had a long, stressful day. We'll be right out."

I shuffled out of there real quick. Not a million miles off what I was used to. Kate was asking Bailey what was wrong, and I didn't want any part of it. As soon as I got in the car, I just closed my eyes and pretended to sleep. The journey home was silent.

Chapter 10

As Monday arrived, I started getting really excited for ballet. I wrote down the teacher's comments on a piece of paper and stuck it in my jeans pocket. Every hour or so, I would pull it out and read it and savor how the words made me feel. I still had to figure out where to get a hundred bucks from. All I really needed was the first ten, and then I'd figure out a strategy.

When I wasn't thinking about ballet or greenbacks, I tried my utmost not to think about whatever had gotten into Tammy on Saturday night. At least she had held it together. No screaming or flying objects. No "let's go nightie-night at Grandpa's". Just nightie-night in Lakewood instead. I tried to figure out what set things off this time and hoped my little boy was OK. I tried to get on top of it. The guilt killed me as I pushed the thoughts somewhere deep, trying to protect myself, but in reality, I wasn't winning.

Josh cornered me at break time as I got some books from my locker. He smiled and brushed the hair out of his eyes. He was such a scruffy kid, but it seemed like the less effort he made, the better he looked. I found myself blushing as he stood there.

"Hey, Alex, how have you been settling in?"

"Hey, how do?"

"Haven't seen you around after school much."

I stared at the ground. "Yeah, no, I guess not." I felt so dumb, not knowing what to say. He was only a little older.

"You know, you can hang out with us after school whenever you like. We go to the pizza place on Madison most days."

I hid my ugly red face behind the locker door and pretended to look for a particular book. I hoped he wouldn't lean in too close and see that my locker was empty.

"Yeah, I mean, it sounds fun, but I'm kinda busy." I closed the metal door, and he stood waiting for me to say more. His face was kind, but all I could think about was Bailey's evil stare and all those horrible rich kids she hung around with. I was better off alone.

"I mean … I guess I'll think about it. Thanks for the offer," I said, and hurried to class. It felt kind of good in a weird way that Josh had spoken to me, seeing as he was so popular and funny and hot and all.

After school, I made some tea and helped Tammy unpack the groceries. We were going through a serious amount of food. She was making three trips to the store a week. Strangely enough, I hadn't gained all that much weight, although though my ass was no longer bony, and my jeans were getting to be a tight squeeze. Maybe I had grown a little.

Tammy went to lie down as I put everything away. I really didn't want to do it, but that was when I had my chance. Her purse was on top of the microwave by the car keys. Even though Old Buck was outside hacking a tree and Bailey was next door, I just went ahead and did it. I closed my eyes and opened my ears and made my move. I whipped the purse open and stared. There were some one-dollar bills, a twenty and a ten.

"Oh, really? Are you sure you didn't drop it at the checkout?" I said to myself, playing out the future scene. I scrunched the ten into my jeans pocket. Then I gulped orange juice from a carton and finished unpacking calmly before retreating to my room. My heart pounded, my senses alive and my mood mixed. What had I done? It didn't matter. I didn't care.

* * *

Tuesday, I was wearing horns. As soon as I got to school, I knew something was up. Kids hushed as I walked by; others just started laughing. Some kids mumbled stuff. I bypassed the biology classroom and swung a left toward the toilets, thinking maybe I had some cream on my face or food between my teeth. I found nothing more unusual than a tiny zit on my chin that was just beginning to throb.

We dissected cow's eyeballs in class. At break time, I needed some air, so I went for a walk by the sports track to clear my head. I passed some tenth-graders smoking. One guy shouted something rude about my butt. A couple of others shouted after me, calling me names.

Another guy took up this incessant wolf whistling. My cheeks burned, and I upped my pace. Someone told them all to shut up and ran after me calling my name.

"Hey, wait up."

"Leave me alone," I said quietly.

He caught up and walked alongside me. He had these crazy big eyebrows and dumb thick-rimmed spectacles that made him look like Clark Kent. I kept walking and stared straight ahead.

"You're Alex, right?"

I changed direction and headed for the athletics track, thinking about doubling back toward the library on the far side. The wind chill was something else, and I pulled my jacket up over my mouth. My sneakers crunched the frozen snow underneath. The kid kept following.

"Listen, Alex, I don't mean to bother you …"

I stared straight ahead and kept walking.

"Wait. Don't you want to know? Look, there's something you need to see."

I stopped dead and grabbed him by his coat. His eyes went fuzzy.

"Stop following me, or else!"

He didn't follow, but I hadn't walked five paces when he called again.

"I bet you're wondering why everyone's laughing at you."

I stopped and turned.

"Do you even know what I'm talking about? Just take a look at this." He stretched his cell phone toward me. "I think someone may have hacked your Facebook."

I grabbed the phone and read. It was a Facebook page in my name with a photo album titled "Kentucky Life: My Family". They were pictures of total hillbillies and rednecks and they had been tagged Mom and Dad. According to the album, I had fourteen brothers and sisters, some of whom were married to each other. Some of the week's statuses said stuff such as me liking boys and girls, especially old granddad guys — I was sweet on them. Today's status update was kinda straightforward. It said, "Hi, I'm Alex and I'm a big whore".

The Facebook page had a picture of me, but it wasn't my Facebook page. The profile picture was of me eating a sandwich on a school bench. I shoved the phone back into his hand and turned to go.

"Hey, I know what it feels like. The guys give me hell the whole time."

I kept walking.

"It sucks to be different."

That caught my curiosity. I turned. "What do you mean?"

"Well, I do Irish dancing."

"Yeah, you probably shouldn't tell people that," I said, and kept walking, before finally shouting thanks over my shoulder.

* * *

I knew where they would be.

They were leaning up against the metal bar under the football stands, almost expecting me. Vanessa smirked, and Bailey, with her creepy green eyes and overdressed face, finished her cigarette and flung the butt at me.

"Shouldn't be surprised, should we, girls? Gonna get yourself in a lot of trouble if you're not careful," Bailey said, all relaxed.

Vanessa sniggered, and Dominique pouted before speaking. "Here comes the hussy."

My adrenaline surged.

"Friendly with the teachers too, I hear," said Vanessa.

I glanced between Dominique and Vanessa. My head began to flutter.

"You're gonna need to leave town, girl," Vanessa continued. "You might not be wanted at home, but you sure as hell aren't wanted here. Just like your mom, aren't you?"

I felt the nails grow on both my hands, a wolf ready to pounce.

Bailey's eyes darted in uncertainty as Dominique and Vanessa inched closer.

"You hear me, redneck?" said Dominique. "You should go on back to Hoosierland. Back to Daddy. You're Daddy's little girl, aren't you?"

I can't say I remember much after that; my mind and body went all automatic and weird. Someone else took over. I can't remember who hit what first, but I smacked Vanessa across the cheek so hard my hand ached. Then someone shoved me to the ground. My hair was being torn out of my scalp. I heard some boys shouting amid the grunting and gouging. I felt warm spittle-breath on my neck as I tried to get whoever it was off of me. Something sharp struck me in the back, and I lay still, barely able to howl, all the breath having left my lungs.

"Get off her! Get off her for Chrissake. Jesus Christ! What the heck?"

I felt a great weight lift from me and heard scampering footsteps.

The tenth-grade bespectacled kid helped me to my feet, cigarette still hanging from his mouth. I could barely stand up straight enough to look him in the eye or thank him.

"Are you OK? Man, did you take a beating!"

I tried to nod. He offered me his cigarette, and I declined as politely as I could.

"What's your name?" I asked.

"Donald."

"Donald?"

"What just happened there?" Somebody whistled, and he turned his head quickly. "Oh no, here comes Mr. Balmer."

I tried to walk, but it pained like hell to put weight on my right foot. The boy helped me hobble toward the school's side entrance. Mr. Balmer, the vice-principal, stood waiting.

"Are you OK, miss?" he asked, neither concerned nor amused.

"I think so," I said with a grimace.

Donald nodded awkwardly. Mr. Balmer's nose started twitching like a bunny rabbit's. The kid glanced nervously at me and left.

"I'm not sure what I saw or didn't see, young lady, but I think we'd better go and have a word with the principal."

"You're kidding, right?" I roared. "You either did see what happened or you didn't." I couldn't quite find the volume setting for my voice.

"Please, miss, try to remain calm. Let's go and have a talk with Mr. Dennaghy, shall we?"

Chapter 11

Old Buck and I sat in the truck in silence for almost twenty minutes while Tammy talked with the principal, both of us silent. I had told Balmer and Dennaghy exactly what had happened. I told them about the Facebook page and begged and begged them to check the Internet. Finally, they did. But there was no trace of a false Facebook page in my name.

Some kind of dumb slide electric guitar music played on the radio. I couldn't take it.

"Can you turn that racket off?" I asked finally.

He turned and looked at me with his beard. "I always say innocent until proven guilty, but when it comes to my music, there's an exception to the rule."

He turned and cleared his throat, then started humming along. A minute later, he glanced back. There was a smile under there somewhere. I grunted and scratched my head with vigor. Tammy came back, and we drove in silence. Then it occurred to me, and I dove my head in front. "Where's Bailey?" Nobody answered me. "Hold up, where's Bailey?"

"At school," said Tammy.

"What? How? Why?"

"Bailey's in class. School doesn't finish until four. You should know that," she said smartly, her lips all self-righteous.

"You are kidding me," I said, or something to that effect.

"ALEX! Watch your mouth!" the big guy shouted.

I saw my mouth hanging open in the rearview mirror. Then I just watched the dumb streets, cradling my hand, biting my lip. Typical.

It turned out I was suspended from school until Monday. I didn't care though; school could go to hell. I stayed in my bedroom all afternoon reading Kate's kitty books for entertainment. It was either that or playing dolls, but the only thing I felt like doing with those things were putting them in the dollhouse and setting it on fire. The image brought flames to my cheeks, and I held my breath instead.

Later, Kate got changed to go practice in the garage. She greeted me with a smile and asked if I wanted to join her. I told her no, except not so politely.

Old Buck knocked on my door and brought me a plate of food. I told him I wasn't hungry. He said, "What about all the starving people in Africa?" I asked him if he knew where the post office was and that I had an envelope he could use. After a while, I couldn't help myself. They were chicken nuggets and fries, sachets of ketchup on the side. I ate them quickly before they were completely cold. They went down quick and necessary.

As seven p.m. approached, my anxiety increased. I opened the bedroom door a little and could hear talking in the kitchen. The TV was on in the living room. At 7:05, I grabbed my sports bag, put on a second sweater because my coat was in the kitchen and crept out the window.

I ran until my lungs burned to escape the cold and was down the road a piece at the Beck Center in five minutes flat. I felt too tired to dance, but happy I had made it.

I had just about finished changing into my shorts when I looked up and saw Old Buck standing there, Kate by his side. A flyer hung loosely from his right hand. Kate must have found it in my room. I turned my back and tried to hide behind one of the others, but I knew he had seen me. I exhaled long and slow. My ass was surely roasted this time.

"Can I help you?" Ms. Allen asked.

I sighed and trudged toward them.

"It's OK, Ms. Allen. He's my dance partner," I said, and made a face at him.

"Well, see, that's where the problem starts," he said slowly. "Looks like I forgot my leotard, so I can't actually practice tonight." Kate held his hand and stood close, face guilty. "I'm afraid I'm going to have to take Alex with me. I'm sorry, ma'am."

The teacher looked at us both.

"Sure, of course, no problem."

Buck saw the sign on her desk and dug his big old hands into his pocket and pulled out some greenbacks.

Ms. Allen waved away his money, took a ten-dollar bill from her deposit box and handed it back to me.

"Maybe next week, then?" she asked. I took the money. Old Buck nodded and ushered me to follow.

I got in the truck, my stomach sick and angry. I snarled at Kate when she turned around. As we pulled into the driveway, Old Buck spoke again, calmly. "Kate, go inside please." She opened the creaky door and got out. "Where did you get that money?"

I felt a lead bomb drop in my stomach. I tried to think of something smart, something believable, but to my surprise, my mouth followed a different route than my brain intended. "I took it from Tammy's purse," I whispered.

I couldn't believe I had told him the truth. I couldn't lie to him, for reasons beyond my knowledge. I wasn't sure if he heard me or not, because he wasn't screaming. I stretched my arm into the front, the note between my fingers. My arm hung there for a moment. "I took it from Tammy."

Finally, Buck turned off the engine and took the money. I braced myself for the earache, but he just opened the door and got on outta there, didn't slam it or nothing. I felt the cold bite me, just like the night they took me away. My tears would have surely turned to ice had it not been for the warmth of my un-smacked red cheeks.

I opened the door quietly and could hear Tammy and Buck whispering in the kitchen. "Where did she get the money from?" she asked.

There was a pause before Buck replied. "I gave it to her. Last week. For helping me in the yard."

My heart hammered inside my chest.

"I'm telling you, I can't take much more of this."

"Come on, Tam, don't be like that."

"Don't you even dare." She spoke the words slowly.

I cleared my throat as I walked through, and she looked at me with bitterness. She hated me, and why wouldn't she? I had been forced into her life, and now she couldn't get rid of me. I rushed by, my face and eyes sore from determination.

The TV blared, and I caught a glimpse of Bailey sitting in the lotus position. A sudden anger hit me. I paused and stood outside the half-open door, blood on my mind, teeth clenched. Then Tammy came down the hall, and I retreated to my room.

A wet towel lay on the ground. I rolled it up and towered above Kate, who was sitting on the floor, reading. I twirled it 'round and 'round, like a lasso, ready to lash out. She winced before cowering, terrified, against the closet door. A solitary tear dribbled down into her mouth, her dimple nowhere to be seen.

"WHY?" I yelled. "How could you have done this to me?"

"Please, Alex, don't." She backwards crawled into a corner, and I edged closer. "I thought you might run away and get hurt." She pleaded with her hands, too afraid to cry any more.

"You little busybody! Because of you and your dumb family, my life is ruined. I should just run away. All I wanted was to go to the damn dance class, Kate! Why can't you just leave me alone? Why don't all of you just leave me alone? I wish you were all dead. I wish you were all dead and gone to hell!"

There was silence. Kate stood up. I felt myself shaking. Color had returned to Kate's face as I panted. She didn't seem scared now. She placed her hand in my free hand, and as if by magic, the tension lifted. I looked at the towel I was still holding and dropped it. My mind was crumbling.

"Please don't run away, please," she whispered, and gazed into my eyes.

"Why the heck shouldn't I?"

"Because I'd miss you. And Mom and Dad would miss you. Mom is already so sad the baby didn't come when it was supposed to. Please don't go."

My mind went snowy. What was she talking about?

"I love you, Alex. Everything will be OK. Promise."

Love? My heart was a jumbled jigsaw. I dropped to my knees and gave her a hug. The door opened, and we parted. Tammy stood there with a grim expression on her face.

"Kate, darling, go into the living room for a minute. Alexandra and I have to talk."

I picked up the towel and hung it on the wardrobe. Tammy sat, mournful. "Alex, John and I talked —" John? John was his name? "—and we decided you can't stay in our home and … and disobey house rules after everything we've done for you. You have lost our trust, Alex. Now, you may not know this, but this family is barely making ends meet, and we just can't cope with much more."

I stared at the wooden floor the whole time, thinking of how ungrateful I was, feeling a little sorry for myself, hating myself. I avoided her stare like a coward. With a deep breath, I pursed my lips and lifted my head. "Tammy, I'm sorry. Really, really sorry. I promise I'll be good. I promise I won't cause any more trouble."

She paused a moment, nodded, and left.

Chapter 12

Friday, I woke up, and I was fifteen. I refreshed Facebook a million times to see if anyone wished me a happy birthday. Finally, my phone rang, and it was Vinnie.

"Sup, rock star?"

"Sup," I replied, almost breaking my face smiling.

"Happy birthday, little lady,"

"Thank you. Jesus, Vinnie, I hate this place. I want to go home."

"Oh, Alex, you ain't missin' much, I reckon."

"Missin' you," I said in barely a whisper. He didn't reply. "So, what's been happening? Have you seen my parents or Lucas? I haven't talked to them since I left. Are they doing OK?"

"Um, yeah, they're, um, all doing OK, I guess."

"Did you see them around? Are they fixing the house?"

"Um, yeah. What you mean, the house?"

"The huge fire? The night I left?"

"Oh, right. That. Yeah, working hard every day."

This was not the way I hoped my boyfriend's birthday call would go.

"Actually, Alex, I gotta go, I'm all out of minutes. Catch you on Facebook later. Happy birthday, girlfriend. Bye."

And he was gone. He said that last part real cheery, but something about the whole thing was off. I wondered if he was seeing someone else.

Being so idle only left me vulnerable to my thoughts. Was it possible that I missed school? Was that even a thing?

Saturday, I couldn't take it anymore. I rummaged around the living room and Tammy's bedroom for something to do. I found some magazines: *OK!*, *Sport America* and *Crochet USA*. Bear-man, I would never have guessed. Bailey had the TV tied up. I couldn't possibly listen to the junk on Kate's iPod. I grunted like a pig when I found out Bailey was having friends over to study and I'd have to go to Kate's dance class again. It was probably a good thing. Bailey and me alone together was not a good idea.

After I had buckled myself into the car, I realized I had nothing to keep me occupied during dance class. I ran back inside. Tammy was on the phone, but her face was all frown. She stopped talking as I passed through. My gut told me something was up. On my way back outside, I shut the hall door lightly, faked closing the front door and crept back to listen. My heart started racing when she said my mom's name. Tammy's voice sounded different. I put my ear to the door.

"Lucas is gonna be OK, right? They're giving him medication? He's with his father? But I thought ..."

At that moment, Old Buck came in the front door carrying logs. Startled, I fell to the ground real awkward, pretending to tie my laces. Then I ran past him back to the car. My stomach was sick with nerves. Lucas was sick, and he needed me. He was probably really scared just with Dad, without Mom to nurse him. Not that Mom was much use. I remembered a time when I was in seventh grade and I was so sick at school a teacher had to bring me home. It wasn't even midday, and Mom had already been drinking. First, she smiled, not knowing. Then, when I told her I was really sick, she just yelled, "God, Alex, go to your room. I don't want your sick germs getting all over me. Go on now." Then I felt really scared for Lucas. Maybe it was really serious. I wanted to know everything, but at the same time, didn't want to know. I couldn't ask Tammy even if I wanted to.

Kate was chirpy as hell, non-stop chatter — something about her crazy teacher, Mr. Legrand. He had gotten so fed up with the kids one day that he just sat under his desk and allowed one of the kids to be the teacher. Her infectious babble just made everything worse. My mind floated around. Tammy finally hauled her fretful face into the car. She gave me a lying-smile in the rearview mirror.

"You got something to read?"

I nodded uncertainly.

The dance class sucked as per usual. Tammy made tea for the other moms, but one lady with silver-black hair just couldn't be satisfied. Tammy must have made her three different cups of tea before she settled down to drink it. Kate told me that this lady had kids of her own. She had been in a car accident, and the two babies died. I didn't feel like laughing at her anymore. Kate said she was crazy in the head, but the other moms felt bad for her.

The class seemed more organized than before. Even Martin seemed different, his head a little more motionless. Maybe this was his game face. He whizzed around, karate chopping with his legs like a samurai. His upper half was rigid, yet his lower half moved like a Tasmanian devil. But he looked so happy. I recognized that look on his face, that euphoria. When I danced ballet, I had that same look on my face. I studied my history book aggressively until class was over.

For the last thirty minutes of class, they practiced some kind of group dance in which four pairs of kids held hands and danced in a circle one way, then back the other, before intercrossing. They totally reminded me of a group of honeybees doing a waggle dance, communicating with one another without words. Just dance. It was weird.

Kate sat in the back beside me on our way home. I tried not to listen, but felt bad about threatening her before. Her sterile mom wasn't offering any support, and I thought, why should life suck for everyone, especially a poor little nitwitted goon like Kate? Her enthusiasm showed no sign of tiring on our moonlit drive. Her flushed cheeks and hair that curled at the front made her look like an elf.

"So next week is the big *feis,* and I know all my new steps inside-out, but I gotta break in my new shoes in time for State, and it hurts 'cause my feet is all blisters. Wanna see?" I politely shook my head no. "State Championships is next month in Cincinnati."

"Cincinnati. Cincinnati. Such a dumb word."

"Mrs. Gallagher says I've got a real good chance. I know all my steps, I just have to remember to concentrate when I'm on stage and not get distracted on account of all the lights and other kids and the judges with the little bells. And that I got to not pay attention to what they write on their notepads, because that means I might have a blank or not see one of the other girls coming my way." She was the next stage in the evolution of mankind, oxygen completely unnecessary to her. I felt my face broaden.

She wasn't done. "And she says there's no reason why I can't be the best in the world because I am the best, just when I concentrate, but I don't even know how to concentrate, I just sometimes forget things, and I don't know how to remember them, and Mom says I got to eat more meat, 'cause iron will help my mind concentrated,"

Tammy glanced at us in the mirror. Something weird occurred to me.

"Why doesn't Bailey dance?"

"Bailey does dance, or at least, she used to …" said Kate. I raised my eyebrows.

"Yeah, Bailey was an awesome dancer. She even won Nationals when she was twelve, but Mom said we wasn't allowed to go to the Worlds because it was too much money, and Bailey just got so mad —"

Tammy cleared her throat rather dramatically, and Kate stopped. Her eyes just kinda looked around; her head remained still.

"Tell me this, Kate. Why d'you like dancing? Do you just do it to win?"

She nodded uncertainly.

"Or do you do it to make other people happy?"

Kate glanced nervously into the front and gave a noncommittal head shake.

Tammy's voice droned. "Dancing is a great way for Kate to keep fit, and it's lots of fun, and it gets her out of the house and living. And you make lots of new friends, don't you, Kate?"

Kate nodded.

I raged for a moment, not satisfied. "Katie, what's the best thing about dancing? Getting dressed up? Wearing a costume?"

She blew a fart noise at me. "No, silly. The best thing about it is how I feel like I can fly around the stage. My feet just do what they want, and it makes me feel like … It just makes me feel like …"

And her gaze just went to another world, and I knew exactly what she meant, as surprised as I was that Irish dance could have that effect. There were no words to describe that feeling. She giggled warm air in my face. It was a cold night, just gone February.

"Well, Kitty Kat. Next time you're on the stage, before the music starts, close your eyes and picture yourself wearing a magician's hat. Picture how amazing it feels to do your moves. Then count to three before you start dancing and go do it. Forget about who is there or remembering your moves; just do whatever it is that gives you the feeling."

Her smile had disappeared, her face completely serious, tongue between her front teeth. She was silent. I had somehow silenced her. She continued to stare at me, and me at her. Finally, I turned my head and watched the cars go by. Seconds later, I felt her hand take mine and squeeze. She held it for the rest of the trip.

Chapter 13

School passed without incident on my first day back, apart from a brief meeting with the principal, at which I was warned about my future behavior. I also ran into Bailey, Vanessa and Dominique as I walked to English class. They avoided my stare. At least maybe now they would leave me alone.

My mind still plagued me about home, about Lucas. Images of my poor little golden boy, sick and scared, worried me no end. Vinnie hadn't been on Facebook and hadn't "seen" the billion messages I had sent. I decided to come straight out and ask Tammy after school, even if it meant admitting to eavesdropping on her conversation. Because I had to know. Typical of my luck, she was working at the old folks' home and wasn't going to be home until late. I picked up the house phone and stared at the large numbers for an age before setting the receiver down once more. Then I just paced around some. There were some weird noises coming from Tammy's room, so I crept up to the door. I thought there were a dozen kids in there, but as I peeked in, I saw it was just Kate. She was rooting through a box of costume clothing of some variety—a red wig, stilettos, belts and feather boas. At least, I hoped it was costume clothing. She was playing out some kind of production with herself: posh woman, police officer and some talking mice. Seemingly, an ancient ring had been stolen from a studio apartment on West 17th and Christmas Street, and the lady was anxious for it to be returned. I snorted with laughter.

"Oh, Mr. Grossman, it's Inspector Lollipop," she said. It turned out I had arrived just in time. Kate handed me a small notebook and a top hat. The famous writer-cum-detective was here to save the day.

Tuesday afternoon, Tammy was out again. I tried and tried to push thoughts of Lucas out of my mind, telling myself it was probably nothing. I didn't even have a ballet class to think about. I sat on a bunch of pillows, staring at homework I had long finished, thinking about how useless and helpless my sucky life was. Kate popped her head in looking for something or other, a frown on her face that I hadn't seen before.

I couldn't help myself. "Hey kiddo?" I halted her progress. "Slow down, you might hurt someone." I forced myself to smile.

"Not right now, Alex," Kate said in a grown-up voice. "I can't find my sock glue, and I need it for the *feis* this Saturday."

"Sock glue? What the heck? You have got to be joking!" I started laughing.

She dropped her chin, and with those blue eyes all fiery and serious, spoke slowly, raising one hand to my face. "Please, Alex, I don't have time for this."

I couldn't help but bust my gut laughing. She looked like actual steam was about to come out of her ears. She stammered, in search a comeback, and ended up punching my arm and walking off.

"Ow! What was that for?"

She slammed the wardrobe and dived onto her knees. I stood behind her as she searched under my bed.

"Listen, Kitty Kat. I'll help you find it. It's gonna be OK!"

"Check the kitchen." Her voice was muffled.

Eventually we found it in a plastic bag in Tammy's room, and Kate's mood lightened somewhat. "Now I gotta practice," she said.

"You want me to come watch?" I asked, surprising myself.

"For real?" she asked, like it was Kentucky-Fried Friday.

The garage was surprisingly warm. Old Buck had covered the concrete walls with carpet and installed a small heater. A workbench ran around the perimeter of the garage, and there were various tools and vice grips and whatnot. There was even a loft space, which housed a load of mechanical junk as well as some old canvas paintings. According to Kate, Old Buckster was quite the Van Gogh in his early years. I climbed up the stairs and grabbed a painting of what looked like fruit sailing down some rapids and almost choked laughing. I placed it over by the stereo and tried to figure out just what it was. Just when you thought you knew an old bearded guy. The loft was the perfect place for Buck's artwork.

Kate clicked her fingers in front of my face and I came back. The majority of the floor space was covered in two layers of chipboard, and there was a stereo system mounted to the wall. First, Kate played some pop music. She grabbed two jump ropes from a hook, threw one to me, bobbed her head to the pop beat, tied her hair tight in a pony, nodded and started jumping. I frowned.

"I said I'd come watch!"

"Do it. It's fun," she said, already panting.

I swung the rope, and it caught my left heel as I jumped. I tried a couple more times, only managing two or three before tripping.

"C'mon, lazy bones, lift your feet."

Kate laughed, and her speed slowly increased as she jumped like a professional boxer.

I concentrated a little harder, sweat beginning to warm my forehead. Soon I got into a rhythm, and I counted off eight in a row before messing up. Then I got to thirteen, and I made it my mission to make twenty in a row, even though the music had stopped and so had Kate. She stretched out her skinny legs.

"I want to work on something Martin showed me that they do in Ireland, but I don't know it all yet, so maybe I'll just work on something else, OK, because we don't have mirrors. I can't see if I'm getting my left leg straight enough when I do this move."

She gave it a weird name that made no sense, then showed me the gist of it, which seemed quite complicated. She showed me what it should look like and what she thought she was doing wrong, both in slow motion and quickly, and even though I knew a bit about dance, it all looked pretty much the same to me. The margin of error was tiny.

"OK, it comes in the second part of the reel, so you'll need to be ready for it.

"Don't worry. I can keep it real."

"No, dummy, a reel is a dance. I'll wink at you when it's coming up."

"Real is the name of a dance? For real?"

"Reels are the best! You do it in your light shoes, and it's a reel 'cause the music timing goes one-two-three-four, one-two-three-four." She sounded like a machine gun. "This reel is my total favorite of all time—*Fairy Feast*. It's from the latest James Mitchell CD."

"James Mitchell CD? What the heck?"

Kate flicked the remote control, and the irritating music began, high-speed chipmunk stuff played on instruments that are probably considered weapons of mass destruction. She used the whole floor space as she danced, turning mid-air, spinning. She was able to get so high on her toes, and all without blocks. She was light on her feet and could get really high off the ground. It was kind of graceful, but in a robotic way. Ballet would probably have been of benefit to her. Then she winked at me, and I squinted, concentrating, and when she did the move, I didn't even have to look close to see if she got it wrong, because her face told the whole story. She continued dancing, her face looking like she had been sucking lemons and chewing pine cones. She stopped suddenly, puffing air. The music continued.

"Again. I gotta do it again."

She was a real never-say-die kid. She waited for the same part of the tune to come back around, took up her military pose and shot off once more. I watched carefully. She winked and proceeded to mess it up even worse than the first time. She kept dancing, but I walked over and pulled the plug on the stereo.

"Hey, what you do that for?"

She looked like a devil-child fresh from a Halloween movie.

"Easy tiger, I just have to tell you something."

"What?" she asked bluntly, and puffed air.

"I reckon your leg is pretty much straight every time you do it. It looks pretty good. Maybe not perfect, but still good."

"No, Alex, it has to be perfect, else I won't win."

"But you're not thinking straight," I yelled, wondering why I was getting frustrated. "Everything you did up until that was perfect. You were like a little butterfly floating around kicking butt." Her face softened. "And it's your dumb, puny face that lets me know you messed up. If you had just kept smiling with those gappy teeth and the big crater in your cheek, I would never have noticed."

112

"You wouldn't notice because you don't know anything about Irish dance."

What a wicked little cat, I thought. I considered leaving, but something stopped me.

"Look, Kate, you're right—I don't know anything, but just remember this: so what? Maybe you mess up that one bit, but everything else is good. Who's the girl that always wins?"

"Samantha."

"Samantha?" I smirked. "What makes Samantha so good?"

"She's got the highest jumps I've ever seen, and she's always got loads of cool tricks in her set dance." She said it so sadly.

"Well whoop-de-doo for Samantha. Let me give you some information about Samantha you may not be privy to, kid. First up, Samantha has a dumb name, and she probably has a dumb face too." Kate's face perked up a little. I became encouraged. "She probably has no friends and does bad in school. Now think about this. What if you only make one mistake, but Samantha makes two? Or maybe three? Will the judges know because they saw her feet, or because her face shouted down at them, 'Oh poop, I just pooped up'?"

Kate held her face as she laughed.

"I'm just saying, Katie, it's hard to get it perfect. If you want to win, you just have to do your best. Samantha might make two mistakes, and you'll win. And anyway, it's not about winning!" I yelled. I grabbed the remote control from her hand, plugged in the stereo, and pressed play. "Do it again, and this time, don't wink at me when it's coming up. I know when it's coming, OK?"

She nodded and went to the center of the floor and began again.

Chapter 14

Vinnie was nowhere to be seen on Facebook, He wasn't replying to my messages, and I was anxious to know what was going on. I called Grandpa a bunch of times, but there was no answer. After that, I decided to just put it all aside and try not to think about stuff. As the week progressed, Kate became a little more nervous, which resulted in a little more focus. She practiced for two hours each afternoon after homework, and I tried to help her any way I could. Sometimes I did some ballet stuff as I watched, wondering how the moves would fit in with the dumb jig tunes. On Friday, we did only forty minutes' work, and as Kate finished up with some stretches, the music continued playing. Feeling particularly energetic, I started doing the over-two-threes that she and Martin had shown me. I even threw in some of the things I had seen Kate do, in jest.

It was good to see Kate smile; she had become so serious in the last few days and hadn't once mentioned the crazy antics of her teacher, Mr. Legrand. Her smile encouraged me to continue, to become more adventurous with my moves. We both laughed. I didn't care how foolish I looked, because it was kind of fun. It was only when Kate stopped laughing and just stared that I became self-conscious. I stopped abruptly, panting.

"What?"

Kate said nothing.

"It's not funny anymore? Is that it?"

She looked like her brain was ticking overtime, but not in her normal zillion-question way. "No," she said.

"Oh, come on, kid, lighten up. I was just fooling around."

She shook her head quickly, making sure I understood she wasn't being negative.

"Alex, that was actually pretty good."

"Oh, shut up!" I dismissed her with a wave and snatched her water bottle. I walked over and unplugged the stereo. When I turned around, she was standing in front of me. She spoke slowly, her eyes wide.

"I'm serious, Alex. That was actually, kind of, what it's supposed to look like."

"Katie, shut your squeaky mouth!" I said sternly.

She shrugged, threw her bag over her shoulder and walked out the garage door shouting over her shoulder. "Suit yourself!" She turned the light off, leaving me fumbling in the darkness, only the red glow of the heater for company. Still, I shivered.

* * *

Friday night, Tammy asked me to keep Kate occupied because she was driving her crazy as she tried to get everything ready for the *feis* the following day. I didn't realize what an ordeal the whole thing was. What I did know was that Kate had been following Tammy around with a to-do list, acting crazy, starting a different chore before finishing the first. She had poor Tammy so stressed out. I took her into Tammy's room to fool around.

First we put on make-up and nail varnish and fixed up our hair. Then we turned the radio on. This dumb song called "These Boots Are Made for Walkin'" started playing, and Kate put on Tammy's high heels and strutted around. I just shook my head, my hair falling into my face, and we danced and laughed. Then I remembered something else, and I felt a pang of sadness in my chest. Or was it anger? Momma and I used to dance to terrible nineties music late at night while we waited for Dad to come home. Often, he didn't. This time it was me who wasn't coming home.

The song ended, and a familiar voice in the hallway broke the memory. It was Vanessa. She was staying overnight with Bailey. I stood at the door listening, holding one hand over Kate's mouth. They were talking about what they would get Brad and Josh for Valentine's Day and what they were hoping to get in return. Vanessa had spent a small fortune on concert tickets for Brad. Bailey said something about trusting Josh and hoping to let the relationship "progress". Dominique didn't have a boyfriend, but she had been flirting with this older guy they kept referring to as Mr. Abs. He was a dancer, apparently. I went to my room and stayed motionless for hours, wanting to eat my own hair and trying not to think about Vinnie and home.

I could have chilled out on Saturday—in bed or in front of the TV—but I decided to go with Tammy and Kate to the dance competition just to replenish my cache of jokes. Tammy was surprised, but I think it made her a little happy. I think Kate was talking me up when I wasn't around.

The *feis* was in Columbus, which meant getting up at 7 a.m. There wasn't anything humorous about that. No one spoke in the morning. Instead, Tammy and Kate went about their tasks in much the same way as dance drills in class. It was very regimental. There was an unspoken protocol being followed as bags and whatnot were packed into the car. Kate rode shotgun, and I squeezed into the back beside her costume bag. I had hoped to get a couple hours' sleep on the way, but Kate insisted on listening to her James Mitchell CD at an unpleasant volume to help her "focus". At that point, had I suffered a terrible heart attack or brain hemorrhage, I would have been happy enough to die.

According to Kate, it was one of the biggest dancing competitions in Ohio, and it was important for her to try out her new steps so that she could have them perfected for State Championships the following month. Maybe she thought she had a chance of winning State. I thought about all the practice and hard work she did. It seemed like such a waste of time. There were better, more important things in life. Kate was too young to perform at the World Championships and would be for another couple years, so in a way, State was like an unofficial World Championships for under-nines. Kate said dancers used this *feis* to get their steps right before going to State. For the older kids, State was their last prep before Worlds.

I rubbed my eyes. Tammy drove around the lot looking for an empty space.

The competition was held in a pretty big theater. When I walked in, I was smacked in the face with the noise, movement and stench of hundreds, if not thousands, of bratty kids and horrible moms milling. I almost turned to Tammy and said we were in the wrong place. The midget kids looked like contenders at a clowns' beauty pageant. It was just all wigs and babies and noise and ridiculous costumes. It was like a rainbow had gotten sick all over the state of Ohio. I couldn't get past it. It was so uncivilized compared with the ballet grades I had to take.

Kate had to wait until the embryo-sized kids took their turn on stage. It was one continuous Irish jig noise followed by another, just endless accordion music, which was nearly making me hallucinate. It was going to be a long day. There was no place to sit in the actual hall, so we had to set up camp in a viewing area above. It was useful because it was close to the warm-up area, but also really noisy. Tammy grabbed my head and scraped sleep from the corner of my eye.

Not long after that, Tammy shoved ten bucks into my hand and told me to go to the concession stand and get two coffees. I brightened up immediately. We sat and watched the fetuses finish up. They looked like miniature rats, drunk, tripping around stage. I nudged Kate and told her so. She suppressed a giggle.

"Hey, Kitty Kat, how the heck are they going to pick a winner out of this garbage?"

She just pouted and nodded. "Wait till you see."

Soon I understood. When it was time to crown the winners, each and every tiny dancer took to the stage and received a medal.

"Oh my God," I said, and pinched the bridge of my nose.

"Oh, come on, Alex. It's nice for the kids to get a reward for trying so hard," said Tammy.

I guess she was kinda right. What frustrated me was the impression these kids would get about life. They weren't going to get rewarded for just trying when they were in high school. Only winners were remembered. It wasn't fair.

As one little girl came back to her mom beside us, her wig came off, and my mouth just dropped real slow. I couldn't believe what I was seeing. This poor little kid was wearing make-up and lip gloss. The older girls had their legs all orange like they had spent weeks in Florida. It was both funny and disgusting. The more I looked, the more ludicrous the whole scene appeared to me, like when you think of a word, and the more you think about it, the stupider the word sounds. I laughing started and laughing and couldn't stop. Kate just stared. It was like a circus except with children instead of animals.

There was so much detail; the only thing that stuck out was anything plain. Some of the dresses were out of control: fluorescent pinks and yellows and greens on black, yellow on white, tartan something or other, migraine. One kid looked like an actual robin redbreast. The wigs weren't all the same either, although they were all curly. Some were almost Rasta-looking, others short, others tied up. I looked hard for a mullet wig — that would have been the coolest. Those wigs were fire hazards. I thought I was going to pass out from laughter, tears rolling down my cheeks. Tammy glared at me, and Kate was, for once, quietly bamboozled.

"What is all this?" I asked, appalled.

"They all do it. It's just part of the competition," said Tammy. "It's easier than rolling it every night and worrying about it falling into your face during a dance."

"But it's a dance competition, not a beauty pageant. And why does it have to be curly, anyway?"

Tammy just shrugged.

"Hey, Alex, wanna come to the warm-up area with me?" asked Kate.

I finished my coffee and nodded, but when I turned to join her, she was already gone. I hurried in the general direction of the chaos.

Unlike Tammy, the other parents weren't shy about yelling at their petrified kids, who seemed ready to crack under the pressure. There were some older kids too, some of them maybe as old as seventeen, dressed to dance, but shouting instructions at younger kids, presumably from their dance classes. I even spotted two cute boys, possibly my age or older, stretching and sipping soda. They were dressed more like ballroom dancers—dark dress pants and shirt tucked in. The warm-up area was crowded with kids from Kate's age group, many who wore dresses that looked like they were made out of a combination of colored aluminum foil on a backwash of fluorescent color. One little girl screamed and ran toward us when she saw Kate. She gave her a giant hug.

"Hey, Sandra."

"Oh my God, oh my God, Kate! Wow, you look amazing! I'm so glad you could make it. How are the new steps? Oh my God, I haven't seen you in ages. What number are you? Are you on with Nicole? Did you see Siobhan's new dress? Are you ready? Have you practiced everything? Are you nervous?"

My mouth hung open. This could not be real. Was it possible for someone to out-hyper Kate?

"I guess."

"You'll be great!"

"Like, Sandra, I guess I've pretty much done all I can, and I just have to try my best, and we'll see what happens, you know?"

She glanced at me, and I suppressed a laugh. She must have been watching too many sports shows with Old Buck. Sandra looked at her with twinkly eyes. All the enthusiasm made my stomach churn.

"I wish I was as good as you!"

"You are good, Sandra."

At that point, another goofball kid came up.

"Oh hi, girls." She was smiling way too much for my liking. "Oh, this is fun! It's like the sleepover gang is reunited. Hey, wanna ask my mom if we can get ice cream after, and maybe we can get pizza later and come back to my house to watch a movie, maybe?"

I jerked Kate by the hand and pushed my way past the two girls. "Sorry, girls, Kate has to go get warmed up now. We'll see you in a little bit."

I walked us toward a free space, Kate pouting. "Hey, what you do that for? Those were my friends."

"Look, I'm sorry," I said unconvincingly. "It's just—" I looked at the clock in the corner "—we have to get you ready to be on stage in, like, less than forty minutes. We need to warm up your muscles, don't we?"

Kate looked back at me. "I guess so."

She spent the next ten minutes jumping around like a lunatic, working up a kid-sized sweat, and then did some stretches. Then she fixated on a particular move, doing it over and over at least a hundred times.

As Kate rested, I hopped around the practice floor, jabbering ballet stuff. "You got to have really strong feet, and lots of times you get these horrible bruises, and the skin gets really hard like cement, so after a while, it doesn't hurt anymore."

She seemed pretty impressed as I pirouetted around. "Let me," she said and tried to copy me.

"No, don't," I lunged for her hand, but it was too late.

Kate landed on the floor with a howl.

"Kate!" I yelled. She jumped up real quick and hobbled for a second, a grimace on her face.

"I'm OK," she said. "Really, it don't hurt that much."

My face boiled. "C'mon, we better get back."

I was totally silent on our walk back to the others, so annoyed with myself. Tammy took Kate to get changed. Even though a similar tune played over and over again, I had somehow learned to block it out. Soon Kate came bounding back, and I felt even worse. It was the first time I had seen her in her competition dress, which was bottle green with orange and white embroidery. Her face was all made up like an adult. Her cute natural curls had been replaced with a ridiculous black, curly wig.

I snorted. "Got your Lucky Charms?" She pushed past me. "Hey, Tammy, let's hope we don't grab the wrong kid when we leave, huh?"

"MOM!" Kate cried.

"If you don't win, Katie, we *will* take another kid home," I continued. Tammy gave me a subtle head shake. Kate huffed and turned her back to me. "Hey, remember what I said to you before: you're good at this because you like it, and it's fun. Don't forget that."

Mrs. Gallagher took Kate and her under-nines to one side and spoke with them before some final pinning of numbers and tactics talk, I guessed. She brought them downstairs, and Tammy and I followed. We found a couple of free chairs down back. The theater was packed with moms, a handful of dads and a whole bunch of crying babies who would no doubt grow up with a distorted impression of reality. Bizarrely, a professional photographer had set up a stall just outside the auditorium.

Tammy started getting real antsy after a bit. She looked this way and that, like a clucking chicken, checking her watch, even biting her fingernails, which was just plain gross. Finally, she handed me Kate's bag and the rest of our stuff.

"What's biting you, Tams?"

"Kate. I have no idea where she is. She's on stage in the next group, and there's no sign of her. It's very unlike her."

"Oh, come on. She's probably just in the bathroom or something. Relax, Tammy."

But she was just all pale and worried and took off to ask Mrs. Gallagher and Mrs. Torso and Mrs. Waffles had they seen Kate. You couldn't lose that kid if you tried. Tammy returned a few minutes later, her cheeks flushed this time.

"So, where was the brat?"

"Just with some of the other kids at the warm-up."

"See. I told ya."

Tammy didn't seem impressed.

Finally, Kate's age group began to dance. They took to the stage three at a time, a keyboard man and an accordion dude playing a familiar tune. All those Irish tunes sounded the same to me, though. They were all the same amount of terrible.

Just before Kate took to the stage, a familiar something pale caught my eye. A couple rows away to my right, I saw a short black-haired woman, and standing about a head taller beside her was Dominique. I nudged Tammy, eyes frozen on Dominique.

"What?" asked Tammy, annoyed.

"That's Dominique over there. What in the name of frozen hell is she doing here?"

"Oh, she used to dance too, but gave up when Bailey did. Her sister is Kate's age."

I tried to process this information, but didn't really have time, as Kate and the other two girls had lined up on stage. She looked a little nervous as she lined up dead center between two taller girls. The music started. She closed her eyes for a second and soon started dancing just like she had in the garage.

Tammy leaned across and whispered, "That's Dominique's sister up there."

My heart beat faster. "Which one? Yellow or blue?"

But Tammy didn't answer, just concentrated hard on Kate's performance. I did too. I waited for the difficult move she had been practicing. She was making sure to keep out of the way of the other two, who flew around as if hell-bent on taking each other out. My heart skipped a little, and I slapped my face softly, told myself to man up. It was just a dumb dance.

Kate performed the tricky part perfectly, and Tammy looked across at me funny.

"What?" I said. "Why are you looking at me like that?"

Tammy shrugged. "No, it's nothing. Just, I've never seen you smile before. It suits you." She smiled. I fumed.

Next thing, just as Kate was dancing at the edge of the stage, the girl in the yellow dress collided with her. She had to put her hand down to stop herself falling, but she got up quickly to finish the step as the music ended.

"Is that the sister?" I asked in a pitched voice. Tammy's hand was over her mouth. "Tammy! The one in the yellow dress?" I asked a second time, firmly. I headed for side stage.

"Where are you ..." she mumbled. I didn't hear the rest. Kate, red-faced, was trying hard not to cry as she came down the steps, the yellow-dress brat behind her. I grabbed Kate, stooped and looked into her eyes.

"Are you OK?"

She was too shocked to respond. Then I confronted the girl. I tapped her shoulder as she walked away.

"Hey, hey, what the hell was that?"

She turned and glared at me. "What's it to you?"

My anger surged, and I pushed her in the chest. I could feel a silence descend around us. "You nearly knocked her off the stage, you little brat. Why don't you be more careful next time?"

The short dark-haired woman scurried toward me, glowering, but she was beaten by Dominique.

"What the hell are you doing, you freakin' hillbilly?" said Dominique.

"You saw what she did. Your little sister is a bitch, just like you," I said. Our eyes locked.

Then Dominique's mom arrived on the scene. "How dare you speak to my daughter like that! How dare you touch her! I'm going to report you to security. Where is your mother?" she asked, Dominique standing stone-faced beside her.

My voice choked, but somehow I managed to spit out a few cuss words before Tammy grabbed a hold of my arm and dragged me away.

"I'm so sorry, Janet, so, so sorry."

"What are you apologizing to her for?" I yelled.

Tammy's face was all concern. She grabbed me roughly and ushered me out of there. I almost tripped over my feet. Tammy cast a guilty glance toward the watching adjudicators. I kept pleading with her, trying to explain, but she just marched me toward the foyer. I turned my head mid-stride and saw a crying Kate being consoled by Mrs. Gallagher. Tammy kept me on her leash until we stood in the parking lot by the minivan. She opened the doors with the electronic key, and we both stepped in, shivering with cold rage.

"But Tammy, she nearly knocked Kate off the stage!"

Tammy's lips were closed like a purse. She held her head in her hands, breathing. Then she clicked open the glove compartment and took out a single cigarette, lit up and started puffing, me just staring, shivering. She began to breathe a little more gently after a few seconds.

"Just stay away for a bit, OK?" She handed me ten bucks. "Go get some lunch in the mall across the street. You have a watch?"

I shook my head.

"Keep an eye on the clock. We'll meet you back here at four, OK?"

We both got out, and she left. A cold fog had descended on the streets of Columbus, and I didn't even have my jacket, which was in the hall. I buttoned up my shirt, unrolled the sleeves and shivered, blaming the world, before taking off across the street, my stomach hungry for justice.

* * *

I forced myself to eat a burger and some fries, then floated around stores checking out stuff I wanted but would never have. I had a couple of quarters left and sat beside a potted plant by a wishing well. There was a telephone booth across from it. I looked at my silver coins and thought hard. Throw the coins and hope? What could I do? I yanked my hair, went into the booth and swallowed hard. I guessed the best option was to call Grandpa's house. I heard the cold hard clink of the coins dropping, a ring tone and the beating of my heart. After eight or nine rings, someone answered, but didn't speak.

"Hello?" I said, my voice barely a whisper. "Hello? Grandpa?"

I could hear someone breathing. I said hello once more. The phone made a noise as my units drained. I looked into my empty palms.

"Hello?" I said one more time, and just as I was giving up, there was an answer.

"Alex? Alex, is that really you?" a little boy's voice spoke, and the line went dead. I cried in the booth for what seemed like an age. When my brain came to, I noticed it was almost four-thirty. I ran across the street to the parking lot, where they had been waiting for me. We drove home in silence. My mind was a muddle, but part of my heart was happy. Lucas. He was OK.

It was weird for Kate not to talk. I later learned she had come eighth, but what annoyed her more so was that Dominique's sister, Nicole, who had intentionally rammed her, had won. What was the point? She had worked so hard, and for what? Eighth in a nothing competition? It wasn't fair. I was no expert in the jig nonsense, but I did know a little about dance, and to my eye, Kate had danced with more grace and precision than Goldie had.

Tammy didn't speak. It didn't take a genius to figure out why. I had ruined her daughter's chances. When I saw Kate ice her foot, I felt like getting sick. That was also on me. It was so weird to receive the silent treatment, and I'm not sure I preferred it. I decided it was best to retire to my dungeon quarters, every inch of which I knew so well.

Kate showered, came into the room and packed her PJs and some other stuff into a bag, her face different, top lip north facing. She didn't say a word. I figured she was going for a sleepover. A knock on the bedroom door sometime later surprised me. Buck came in and sat on the end of my bed.

"Alex, I know Tammy is mad with you, but I don't want you to worry about it." I didn't say anything. "Look, I know you were trying to do the right thing, sticking up for Kate. You can be so sweet sometimes, but, man, you've got a nasty sting on your tail." He said it with a smile, and insisted that I come have dinner with him and Tammy in the kitchen. I took my time going out there, and they both stopped talking as soon as I entered.

The air was kinda icy, no question. Buck tried to make small talk with me, while Tammy just stabbed at her food. Finally, she pushed her plate away and left. Buck did his beardy-smile thing at me. My face wanted to smile, but couldn't.

I finished up eating and went back to my bedroom and just lay there, the room quiet, the abundance of oxygen keeping me awake. A noise startled me a couple hours later, and I jumped to attention like Pavlov's dog. I opened the door a crack. Tammy was sobbing in the living room. Buck must have been trying to hush her, but I could almost hear her tears drop. I felt just shitty. I was just bad news, and no matter what I did, I dragged anyone who cared for me through the dirt. No wonder Mom and Dad didn't want me. I was starting to accept that my miserable fate had been written in cold stone by God.

Chapter 15

When I woke on Sunday, the snow had vanished. The ugly blue-gray that dirtied the streets had gone, and a tired Earth had emerged. I felt much the same. I needed some sun. Winter had been long, and spring was still weeks away.

The house was empty. Maybe they had decided to go to church and ask the big guy to help solve all their problems, although I wasn't sure if they believed. I often thought about God, whether he existed, and if he did, why he had it in for me so bad.

There was a note on the kitchen table next to a brown cardboard box of fresh bagels—cinnamon, nutty, seedy, plain, little tubs of peanut butter, cream cheese, honey, blackberry jam, garlic butter. "Help yourself!" I sat smiling at the toaster, listening to the coffee percolate.

After breakfast, I wandered the house in search of nothing in particular. I stared at the photos in the hall, family portraits, school plays. I was hyper and bored — the coffee. I needed a walk. I didn't even brush my teeth before I left, eager to go before everyone returned. I'd made it half a block when I remembered. I turned back and scribbled a quick note and set off again.

I passed a park. There was a whole bunch of trees I hadn't noticed before. The trees seemed to say, "Just you wait, Alexandra. The leaves are coming. Then you'll see". I snorted. There was an outdoor swimming pool, which was covered. I grimaced. It seemed like it would be forever before things got better, until the sun came out. I was thinking too much. I wondered what Mom, Dad and Lucas were doing. Maybe spring had already arrived in Kentucky. Maybe they had gone for a car ride to the waterfall, or hiking up the hills with a picnic. Or maybe they were just yelling. I drove the thoughts from my mind.

I stopped by the coffee shop on my way home. It was busier than last time. The girl from before recognized me and smiled. We just stared for a moment, no need to make dumb small talk. I realized I was staring at a little stud in her nose and blushed.

"Wow, your hair got long quick," she said.

I pushed my hands through it and laughed nervously.

"Do you put color in it? It's so blonde."

I just shook my head. "You should see it in summer. It's like the sun—you can't stare directly at it or you'll go blind!" We both laughed, and then I got awkward. I placed *The Catcher in the Rye* on the counter by the tip jar. My face got all warm.

"I'm really sorry. I guess I got a little too absorbed in it."

She giggled. "Oh, no, that's cool. It's a great book. Don't worry about it." She then held out her hand. "Ellen, but my friends call me Nellie."

I shook her hand and laughed. "Ha, Alexandra. Alex. My friends … the same."

A pang of sorrow kicked me in the chest. I shook my head.

"That's a real pretty name."

"Thank you," I whispered. "Yours is awesome."

"So what can I get you, Alexandra, or guess I should call you Alex, now?"

I smiled. "Actually, I don't have any money. I just wanted to return the book."

Nellie waved her hands. "Oh, don't worry about it. Let me get you something. My treat." She nodded at a tall guy behind the counter who was putting a tray in the oven. "My boss always lets me treat friends."

My face lifted. "I'll just take a latte, if that's OK?"

She had already turned away and was soon emptying the metal coffee container, grinding fresh beans.

"Take a seat," she shouted. "Grab a book and relax, and I'll bring it right over."

I did like she suggested, slouched into the same tan beanbag I sat in the first day. I drank my coffee and weighed everything up, how things had progressed since the last time I was here. I had so much energy in my heart, I just wanted to explode. I needed to know what was going on. Sure, I had heard Lucas's voice, but it wasn't enough. I pulled out my phone and saw that Vinnie was online.

"Call me NOW" I texted. Ten seconds later, he called from his mom's cell.

"Everything all right, pretty lady?"

"No. You've been lying to me. I know when you're lying."

"Who told you? Michelle?" he asked, kinda nervous.

"When was the last time you saw Lucas? Is everything OK?"

"Oh, right," he said, kinda accepting. He sighed. "OK, Alex, it was your birthday—I didn't want to make it suck any more than usual. But there's a couple things you need to know."

I immediately regretted asking. "Go on …"

* * *

Only Tammy was home when I got back. The house was so quiet without Kate. Bailey had gone off with her friends, and Buck was off doing bear stuff. I paced around the house, unable to settle. Telling myself that everything was going to be all right was not working. I was close to biting my nails. Finally, I couldn't take it anymore. I went looking for Tammy.

I had to be real careful as I climbed down the creaky basement stairs. Moths would even have trouble hitting the light bulb in the center of the room. It reeked of sweet chemicals. Tammy cleaned fuzz from a filter. There was a drum kit, amp and guitar on the opposite side of the room. I called her name, and she jumped round. I just stared at her, my face blank. She stared back. Neither of us spoke for a minute.

"Tammy?" I said softly. Her face changed. Several seconds passed before I croaked again. "Can I please call my mom?"

Tammy looked back at me, sad, and shook her head slowly. Anger started building inside me, but before I needed it, Tammy spoke again. "I don't have Dorothy's number. That's where they're staying until the house gets fixed. I called your mom, and she says everything is OK and that she'll try to call when she gets a chance."

I shook my head. Mom didn't even have a phone anymore. "No. No, Tammy, you are lying to me."

"Excuse me?" she said, all offended.

"You better start telling me the truth. I was talking to Vinnie."

She sighed and dropped the laundry basket to the floor. "Alex, I'll tell you what I know. I talked briefly with your father. Your mother is sick and is getting some help. She's getting better, but there are some issues with the insurance company and fixing up the house."

"Stop lying to me, Tammy. There's nothing wrong with the house. Vinnie said he cycled by and there was only some minor damage in the kitchen."

"OK, OK. Alex, you need to understand. We are just trying to protect you. We don't want you to worry."

"Spit it out, Tam. It's because she started drinking again, right?"

Tammy nodded. "Your mom had to spend a few days in the hospital, and now she's taking something to help her through it. She's resting up at Dorothy's. Soon enough, everything will be back to normal, and you can go home. We're just not exactly sure when. And your father and Lucas are staying with a friend of his called Mac …"

"I thought he was at Grandpa's? Lucas is with Dad?" Tammy nodded.

I dropped my head to my chest and thought.

Tammy rubbed the side of my arm. "Things aren't so bad here, are they? You just have to take it one day at a time. You're just going to have to try to make the most of things."

She carried her laundry basket upstairs, leaving me with a sinking feeling in my gut. I couldn't help things back home, not from here. I couldn't speed things up. The only way I could make time go faster was to distract myself.

I changed into my sweat pants and sneakers and went across the yard to the garage. I jumped rope for a bit until I felt a sweat form on my brow. It was cold without a fire. Then I played Kate's CD and tried to work on my over-two-threes and fit them with the music. I did them over and over again, biting my lip, doing them faster than necessary. I danced with my eyes closed, focusing on the music, matching the beats with my movements. Soon I was sweating so hard I had to strip down to my undershirt. Without realizing, I had started improvising, thrashing my feet trying to copy Kate's moves, not caring how wrong they were. When my legs began to ache, I danced harder. When my tongue got dry, I danced faster. When my undershirt stuck to my skin, I tore it off and danced in my bra, not caring if anyone walked in. When I couldn't dance another beat or stand another note of music, I kept going some more. Before I left the garage, my eyes rested on Old Buck's painting by the stereo. It didn't look so bad.

I showered and sat on the couch as my hair dried in the warmth of the fire, totally empty. Then I dozed.

Kate came home shortly after, but made a point of avoiding me, leaving the room when I entered, not responding to anything I said or asked. I sat in the living room reading my new book, *Vernon God Little*, which Nellie had lent me. The blazing fire scorched my toes. It got dark at six now, the marginal stretch in the day bringing hope. I couldn't believe it when I heard music from the garage. Even though there were still weeks to go before State Championships, Kate didn't take a single rest day. She had also decided to practice without me.

I thought about how she must have been hurting, coming eighth after all her hard work, seeing Nicole on podium number one. Dominique's pale bitch-face sprang to mind, and I felt so angry.

I decided to go out there after a while. I opened the door, allowing the accordion music to seep out. Kate grimaced and stopped dancing.

"Hey, Katie," I said, smiling gently.

"What is it, Alex? Is dinner ready or something?"

"No, I just wanted to watch you dance."

"Why?" she asked bluntly.

"Reckon I kinda like watching. Because you're good at it." Kate continued to loosen her ankles, but had turned to face me. "Reckon I kinda like dancing too." Her face softened a tad, and I grasped the opportunity. "'Cause maybe someday, I'll be as good as you."

"I'm not good. I only finished eighth," she said sadly.

"Well, it's got to get better, 'cause it can't get no worse."

With that, I started jumping and kicking my heels around the small floor, mimicking Kate's moves, my back straight, arms tight against my hips. Kate just stood there laughing, eventually doubling over, the hilarity too much. I stopped panting and laughed with whatever air remained in my lungs. Then she came over and hugged me tight around my waist before looking up at me with those amazing blue eyes.

"Alex, you are such a dummy. But that was close to being good."

"Oh, come on. You know I'm just trying to cheer you up. Just play along."

She looked at me dead serious. "Honest, if you just went to class, you'd get it real quick. You're good. You have good timing and great carriage."

I blew my lips together. "Whatever! OK, let's get back to your practice. Which one are you doing? The single jig?"

"Phfft! The single jig is for babies. I'm practicing my hornpipe. I have to get everything right, 'cause Nicole got better than me at the last *feis*, and, well, at State, I won't just be against her. Samantha will be there too, probably. Lots of the girls from other states who are too young for Worlds will be there…"

I nodded. "Nicole! You don't need to worry about her. She got lucky that time."

Kate looked away from me shyly, remembering.

"Is Nicole your friend?" I asked.

She didn't answer straight away. "Yeah, she's a nice girl. She is my friend," she said timidly. "She can be kinda Miss Bossy sometimes. Are you friends with Dominique?"

My mind went blurry screaming no to myself. I had done enough damage, and I did NOT want to introduce this cute kid to any more hatred at such a young age. I did NOT want to corrupt.

"Kate, let me tell you something. I personally don't think Dominique is a very nice person, but that's just my opinion."

"Why?"

"Dominique is mean and nasty and doesn't play nice with other kids and makes fun of them and is a bit of a bully."

Kate made this stupid toothy smile and covered her mouth, but I could still see her one dimple.

"So you mean she's a bitch?" She started giggling manically.

"Jesus, Katie, where did you learn that word?" I chased her 'round the room. She squealed as I caught her and tickled her belly.

"Where did you learn that word?"

"I heard Mom say it when she was driving one day and this old lady almost hit us in the car."

I nodded to myself. "Well, don't let me ever hear you say it again, OK?"

She looked up at me all innocent and nodded.

"OK, let's practice. Show me what I have to look out for."

Kate moved back a couple of steps and drew a big breath. I was glad not to have to look at her dumb wig. Her natural hair was much prettier.

"OK, in this one, I need to do my circle around and then cut over back and front like this." She demonstrated. "This is the bit that's hard, because you have to do it quick, and sometimes I forget to pick up my left leg at the back. And in this part, I'm not turning my two feet out enough."

She did it slow, then quick, and I could see immediately where she was having trouble. I had a vague idea of how to get her to do it right, but I asked her to show me in slow motion a few more times until I had it imprinted in my brain.

"OK, I got it," I said finally. "Do it with music now."

Kate looked back and smiled. She extended the remote control, but delayed hitting play. "Hey, maybe after, I'll show you something different as well as the over-two-three, and you can practice that for a bit?"

I thought for a moment, not really sure if I had any energy left, but her face was so hopeful, I didn't want to disappoint.

"Yeah, sure, we can do that."

"OK, great," she said with a skip from one foot to the other. Then the music came, and practice commenced.

Chapter 16

School sucked so much that I had no choice but to listen and learn. We did spring tests. I had never done well in school before, but my grades were turning out pretty good. I got a C minus in math even though it was all geometry, stuff I'd only started to learn. I got mainly Cs and Bs in the other subjects, except for English, in which I got an A minus, but the test was pretty easy. Some of the questions were based on one of my favorite books, *Of Mice and Men*. It was even more pleasing to see Bailey's sourpuss when I got a special mention from the English teacher, Mr. Gonzales. Everyone made fun of Mr. Gonzales because he was from Mexico. But he was so smart.

I had zero interactions with Vanessa and Dominique during school now except for when they tried to destroy me with death-eyes any time I passed them in the corridors. Josh continued to smile and wave and say hi as always. Bailey could neither smile nor give death-eyes, and I actually felt a little bad for her, even though she was nothing but a stupid emo. The reason for that was what happened Sunday night. I was in the kitchen making tea when there was a knock at the door. Josh came in and asked if Bailey was home. I told him she was in her bedroom, and he said "Oh", and his face got all disappointed. Then he said, "I was hoping you would say she was out." It was weird. I had no idea what he meant by that. I just figured he wanted to leave her a surprise or something.

Moments later, as I sipped on my tea, I heard something smash in Bailey's room, followed by screaming. I sat on edge, the terror bringing back haunting memories. Seconds later, the bedroom door slammed, and Josh rushed past me without saying goodbye.

Tammy spent much of the evening on the impossible task of consoling Bailey. I figured they had broken up.

Monday after school, I bought a cute card for Vinnie and made Tammy drive me to the post office.

Tuesday, Josh joined me at my solitary table and sat with me through lunch. I didn't want to ask him straight out what had happened, and he didn't mention it. He seemed fine about everything and was in a pretty fun mood. It felt good to talk to someone my own age, not that there was anything wrong with Kate. I guess I just missed my own friends and Vinnie.

"I just got the new Mighty Dot album. Have you heard it yet?"

"Who the heck are they?"

"They? Jesus. You've never heard of Mighty Dot? They are a she, by the way. Didn't you say you like XO?"

"Yeah," I said, my eyes locked on his giant hazels.

"Well, this gal is at least seven times better."

Josh was handsome. Maybe not so much handsome, but pretty, like a girl. It was weird. He was smart and witty. We had similar tastes in books and music, and he said he would lend me some new CDs he thought I might like. He told me about an outdoor concert in mid-April that was being held at the park bandstand. It was for up-and-coming bands. He was the singer in a band called The Wild Slices. I laughed, and he got a little offended, but he looked even cuter with sore feelings. I punched him in the arm and told him to stop being such a girl.

The following day was the same. I sat at my regular loner table, and he joined me. Some of his friends came and asked us if we wanted to go to the pizza place, but he told them he'd catch up later. He then kept dropping hints about this lame Valentine's night school dance they were all planning on going to the following night. I was not at all tempted.

After lunch, I sat in class and found myself losing concentration as Josh's face kept floating into my mind. He was really sweet and was always complimenting me and laughing at my lame jokes. I wanted to savor the images and feelings and feel good about myself, but the echoes of Bailey's cries combined with the haunting image of Vinnie's to-die-for smile bludgeoned me constantly.

At one point during class, Ms. Jones called my name. She must have called it a couple of times, because I looked up and felt everyone's eyes on me. I felt all woozy. I shook my head from side to side. Ms. Jones asked me the question once again. The words didn't register. I cleared my throat. "Sorry, what's the question?"

"Alexandra, for the third time, will you take that hat off?"

Had I been sunbathing directly next to the sun, my face would not have been as red. I scrunched my eyes and closed my ears to the laughter. I put my hat in my bag. All the faces laughed, except Bailey's. I wanted to hide forever under the table.

Thursday, I woke up semi-hopeful that the mail had come and there would be a card waiting for me from Vinnie. There wasn't anything except a lame-ass Facebook message saying "Love ya, Darlin'". I left for school with a weird knot in my stomach.

Josh and I hung out again at lunchtime, and toward the end, he asked me if I wanted to hang out with him over the weekend. I was on my way to geography, and my mind reeled as he said the words, all nervous, yet charming and adorable.

"Alex, do you think, I mean, would you like to hang out? Over the weekend? I mean, if you're free and all."

I just stuttered, not actually saying anything, leaving the poor guy in turmoil. "I have to go to class," was all I managed, and I ran into the room, my mind ablaze.

Chapter 17

Later that day, I felt all light-footed, and I kinda bounced from room to room despite the fact Vinnie hadn't sent me a card. How would he even get my address in Cleveland, I figured. I was in the kitchen making myself an egg-salad sandwich when I saw Old Buck struggling with bags. I opened the door for him and helped him put the food away. I asked him if he was having a good day, and he looked at me weird and said, "Should I get a doctor?"

Even Tammy remarked. "What's gotten into you? I haven't seen you like this in ... ever."

I just smiled. Soon Bailey arrived, face like a dragon. I got straight out of there in case she burnt me to a crisp.

I made out a countdown chart for Kate on a big sheet of paper and hung it out in the garage. I figured she would need to have her hornpipe down to perfection about ten days before State so that she could dance it in her sleep if she wanted to. I also thought she would need to start eating a little more, because she told me she wanted to up her training by a half-hour each day two weeks before the competition. The poster was mainly cartoons, sketches and words, with a few tables all in different colors. She loved it. She started humming a familiar song as she read the poster, and then spun around, wiggling her shoulders, doing this crazy disco dance. I stared blankly. Finally, she stopped and burst into giggles, covering her mouth.

"My teacher, Mr. Legrand! He's so funny. Yesterday, he put this song on that went, "Ah, ah, ah, ah, stayin' alive", and just like magic, all the kids in my class stood up and started dancing. It was so funny. At first, he stood there with a what-the-heck face, and then *he* started dancing!"

"Hilarious, I'd imagine," I said bluntly. "Hey, you wanna see good dancing? Check this."

I showed her how good my over-two-threes were.

"Wow, Alex, you have those almost perfect now. I think you should just enroll in the class and take it up properly."

"No way, Kate. This is just something me and you do for fun. I wouldn't be seen dead doing this dumb dancing!"

She mucked up her face and stuck her tongue out. "OK, now to the hornpipe!" she said with a lilt. She hammered out some steps, and it all looked pretty concise to me. Then I started finding it hard to concentrate. Josh's face kept drifting into my mind. I thought about how he had laughed when I tried to burp "The Star-Spangled Banner".

Then Vinnie's face took over, and I felt bad. But just for a minute. What difference did it make? He didn't even send me a Valentine's card. I changed my focus quick.

"That looked good," I said.

"Thanks, but there are a few little problems. Look at this. I can do the click on its own, but in the move, I sometimes miss it."

Kate showed me, and I saw what she meant. There were so many combinations, it was no wonder she might miss a piece, but I had no idea how to help her correct it.

"Maybe it's just 'cause your feet are still growing and the muscles aren't strong enough yet?" I suggested.

"Maybe," Kate replied. "I'm going to try again. Just tell me how it looks."

My upbeat mood returned as I watched her practice, so dedicated—one objective, one focus, one ultimate reward—and I thought to myself, when I danced ballet it looked pretty and it felt nice, but this heavy clapping was something else entirely. This was working her rage.

Later that evening, I ate alone as Bailey left for the dance and Tammy and Buck took Kate to something or other. As I finished putting away the dishes, there was a knock on the door, and it was Josh. He had a small package wrapped in red paper with a card taped on top. The two of us stood awkwardly for a moment.

"Bailey's gone to the dance already," I said, but Josh's face didn't change. He didn't say anything, just stepped inside and closed the door.

"Actually, Alex, it was you I wanted to talk to."

My heart fluttered.

Josh stood with expectant eyes. "I—I had to come and ask you, Alex. My brain is fried. And I just need to know one way or the other if ... if you like me back."

And I guess what happened next was born out of frustration and my brain coming to terms with things. It started calm and composed. "Josh, you're a nice guy. I like you, you're fun to be with, you're cute." But then my brain flooded with images of Lucas, Dad, Mom, Kate, my dog, Vinnie, even Bailey, Tammy and Old Buck. "But God, Josh, what the hell are you thinking? What's going through your head? You were dating my cousin up until a few days ago, and yeah, I hate her, but now you want to date me? You're asking me out on Valentine's Day? We live in the same house! Did you even consider Bailey's feelings? Jee-sus! Man, you're so stupid! We've been friends for like a day! How can you be so selfish? Not that it matters, but that's not even the kind of guy I'd want to date, or even be friends with, you know?"

I think there may have been spit coming out of my mouth. I may have been shouting.

Josh's face was ashen. He just stood there with the gift in his hands.

"Leave, Josh!" I opened the door for him. "Don't call us, we'll call you, OK?" I tried to slam the door, but it caught on his heel, so I slammed it a second time. I ran to the bathroom. I'm pretty sure Josh was crying. Why had I stuck up for Bailey? She was a horrible person. It may have even been good for me to hang out with Josh until it was time to go home. I didn't know what to feel. I looked at my teary face in the mirror, but it wasn't me; it was Kate looking back. Not the cute, dimpled girl, but the steely-faced kid who flung her body 'round the floor, driving out the anger through her feet with beautiful precision. I went and lay down in silence, but the damn remnants of an Irish jig swam in circles, refusing to leave my head.

Chapter 18

The following morning, as I gathered my books for school, I was set upon by a wild cat. I was on my hunkers packing my bag, when all of a sudden, someone gripped my ponytail and yanked. I howled and tried to lash out, but Bailey just pulled harder and covered my mouth. I called out, but it was hopeless. She crept up into my ear.

"You're ruining my life, you freakin' hillbilly. Why? Just because yours is messed up? You're trying to steal my boyfriend? And you'd better stay away from Kate! You have no idea what you're putting Mom through."

Luckily, at that moment, Old Buck's big booming voice called for us to get in the car, and she released her grip. I winced and fell forward. I looked back toward the door, my mouth forming words that did not sound until she was gone. "I—but I didn't—I—let me explain, I did, I didn't..."

How did she know what had happened? I couldn't concentrate at school and seemed to run into either Bailey or Josh at the end of every period. Somehow, I

151

made it through the day without getting in any more trouble.

Thankfully, school was shutting for midterm that weekend, because Bailey, Vanessa and Dominique had been giving me serious dead stares. I was looking forward to chilling out on my week off until Tammy notified me of something horrific Monday morning. She wanted me to help out the Irish dance group with a fundraising flash mob due to take place at the end of the week in the local mall. It was for the girl called Rachel, who was in my grade, although I had never spoken to her. She had been diagnosed with leukemia. It was sick, like a John Green book come to life. Her family was pretty broke and needed help with the hospital bills. Rachel used to dance a lot and was in a different Irish dance class from Kate's. She also danced hip-hop. The Irish dance teacher and hip-hop teacher decided to team up and perform a short piece. Rehearsals had already been underway for two weeks. Bailey had been part of the flash mob, but I had noticed she had been limping around the house, breathing fire. I was to be her replacement. I protested, but it made no difference. Tammy played everything except the cancer card to guilt me into doing it.

"Tammy, this is a really important cause and all, but I just don't think it's right to put me in there. If I mess up, they might not make enough money to save that poor girl's life. I mean, you've seen me — I don't even know my left from my right," I said, and pretended to walk

straight into a door. "I want to help out, I do. It's just …
Hey, I'll help collect the money, shaking the buckets and
all."

"I promise, Alex, all you need to know for this in your
over-two-threes. It's just that and skipping around a
little. It's a no-brainer. I promise." She stared at me all
open-eyed and manipulative.

"I don't know, Tammy."

"Mom's right. It's real easy and lots of fun. Do it. Do
it!" said Kate, smiling.

"Shut up, Kate!" I barked.

"If you do this for me, Alex, I promise to make it
worth your while," said Tammy.

"What you mean, Tam?" At that moment, with her
smiling at me, I hated her so much. Then she just walked
off. "Tammy, what you mean by that?" I yelled after her.

Kate giggled and bit her fist. I chased her down the
hallway and smacked her in the butt.

Rehearsals were just two hours a day. They were held
at the schools arts center, which was new and awesome.
It was just the Irish dancers Monday. When we arrived,
Kate headed straight over to Martin, leaving me
standing on my own like a dumb-ass. I recognized some
of the kids from seeing them around school, and was
kinda surprised to see the Clark Kent glasses kid
warming up in a corner. He came toward me, saving me
from loserdom.

"Don't I know you from somewhere?" he asked with
a fake squint.

"Yeah." I smiled. "You saved my ass ... a couple weeks ago."

"Oh yeah." He held out his hand. "Donald. But you can call me Superman." He raised his eyebrows as I shook his hand. "So whatever happened to you after that?"

I laughed, even though it wasn't funny. "I guess I kinda got suspended."

"No way! Man, that sucks. And what about the other girls?"

I squeezed my lips together and shrugged.

"Nothing? You mean they got away with it? That's total bullcrap." He kept pushing his bangs behind his ears. The rest of his hair was short at the back. He was doing pretty bad with acne, and his face was kind of weird. It was almost like all his features were put on a little crooked. And then he smiled. And everything just lit up. Poor guy—his smile was his only saving grace.

We went through the routine to a crappy, upbeat pop track. For once, Tammy was right. It wasn't so bad. I learned the whole thing Monday, which was good, because the flash mob was in four days, and we still hadn't combined it with the hip-hop dancers. There were twenty of us in total. I recognized Lucy from Irish dance class. Others were friends of Rachel's who had never danced before but wanted to help out. Some were even more un-coordinated than me, and I found myself having to explain the steps and movements, which were simple group dances, dancing right in a circle holding hands, then center, then left, with some kids weaving in and out. Ms. Gallagher wasn't one for creative flair. Donald told me that it was just old Irish *céilí* choreography.

By Tuesday, we had it drilled pretty good, which left Wednesday and Thursday to get it right with the hip-hop dancers. In a way, I was almost glad for the distraction, because midterm was boring, and I had fun with the other kids. Bailey was home the whole time, and Tammy was strung out. I was also really curious to see what she meant by making it worth my while.

On Wednesday, I arrived at rehearsal with a smile. The hip-hoppers were there, all dressed and funked up. They strutted around like they owned the place. Even their teacher looked like a total up-his-own-butt jerk. The girls wore cut-off shirts or tight-fitting tops that showed off their midriffs. The few guys wore vests and were pretty athletic. They all wore high-tops and some kind of beanie or baseball cap. I felt stupid. There I was, wearing a plaid shirt, jeans and sneakers.

I caught one guy checking me out as I walked across the floor. He was wearing a leather vest and was totally jacked. He was maybe eighteen, and his arms were like cannons. He had one of those big, square cartoon jaws that some people might call handsome. I guess the more I stared, the more I fell into the category of "some people".

Before we started, the hot guy came over and left his bag down by mine and started talking to me.

He stretched out his hand. "Rob."

With an amount of uncertainty, I shook it and possibly uttered my name.

"Irish or actual dance?" he asked.

"Um, Irish, I guess."

He took a water bottle out of his bag and mixed in a sachet of some kind of powder. "Damn shame, just a damn shame."

"Oh, it's not my favorite type."

"Poor kid. Such a damn shame. Why's stuff like that gotta happen someone so young?"

"Oh, right. Yeah. Rachel. Of course."

Then he faced me, sipping his water, and retied his track suit. I could have been drooling, I'm not sure. I told him I wished I was part of the hip-hop group. He started telling me that I should join. There were classes on Saturday mornings in such and such a place. He wasn't much for smiling—pretty serious—but a nice guy. I wasn't really listening, just gazing. Then the double doors burst open, and in walked Vanessa and Dominique dressed like total skanks. Vanessa just wore a low-cut shirt. Her frame was real slight, so it looked like she had breast implants. I felt pretty inadequate. She wore luminous green baggy pants and a cap. Dominique wore a mini skirt. You could practically see her panties. I felt some vom at the back of my throat. She also wore an oversized baseball cap that looked ridiculous on her.

"Sorry we're late, teacher," said Vanessa, all cutesy. They saw me staring at them, and their eyes did cartwheels from me to the hot guy beside me, contempt written all over their faces. I felt like walking straight out of there as the happiness evaporated from my body. Then they came straight toward us.

"Hey Rob," they said almost in unison.

"We see you've met the hillbilly here. You gonna line-dance?" asked Dominique. The three of them laughed. I took a sip of water and excused myself.

The Irish dancers stood aside and watched the hip-hoppers do their routine to the same music; the whole thing lasted about three minutes. Then we got to work setting the two groups up in the same space and aligning the movements. It wasn't that hard, because the Irish dance lines were straightforward, moving in and out, with some weaving; the hip-hoppers were able to link in and out of their own intuition. They had some cool bits, especially when Rob lifted Vanessa and spun her around. I wished it was me he was lifting. I thought my interactions with Vanessa and Dominique were through for the day, but it turned out there was still time for them to comment on my moves. They said something like I didn't have a beat in my body, and as I watched their cool moves, I felt like such an idiot. If only they could see me do ballet.

Things were still not completely together by Thursday, so we agreed to meet for one hour Friday morning before going to the mall. After I showered, Tammy handed me a cup of tea as I sat by the fire with a towel wrapped around my head.

"So how's it going?" she asked.

"I guess, Tammy, the whole affair pretty much sucks, you know? But I'll live."

She smiled warmly and said nothing for a minute. Then the phone rang. She sat down and said, "Alex, will you get that, please?"

I just gesticulated and grunted. "But you're closest to the phone!"

It kept ringing, and she didn't budge. Finally, I accepted defeat.

"Hello? Buckman residence. How do? How may I be of assistance?"

There was a giggle on the other end. Finally, "Boy, Alex, you sound funny. That's some crazy words for answering the telephone."

"Lucas!" I screamed down the phone, and then my breath snagged and I had to force myself to exhale. I looked around at Tammy's smiling face. My little boy was spouting more gibberish, but I couldn't really take it in.

"How are you, Lucas? Do you miss me?"

"Sure I miss you, Alex, except Grandpa says you'll be coming home sometime soon, and I can't wait, especially if what Dad says is true, that I might be getting a pony."

He was cut off by someone standing next to him, and then I heard the receiver changing hands.

"Hi, Alexandra."

"Grandpa! I miss you. What's happening? How's Mom and Dad and Lucas?"

"Well, as you can tell, Lucas is just fine. He had pretty bad flu for a while. Your mom and dad are doing fine. We're hoping to get you back in six weeks, maybe."

"Six weeks? Yes!"

"We are gonna have to go now. I have to bring Lucas to daycare. Heard you've been getting in a bit of trouble."

"Oh, not so much, Grandpa. You know me."

"OK. Take care. See you soon, Alexandra."

And then he was gone, and I looked at Tammy, my eyes all cloudy with tears. She stood and came over. Then we hugged.

* * *

Friday, I floated around, happier than I'd been in an age. In eight weeks or so, I'd be back home. Thinking about rehearsals and flash mobs didn't bother me once.

We had a quick run-through at the hall at 11 a.m. Friday morning. Everything was pretty tight. Then out came the costumes. The Irish dance girls wore short black dresses. I already hated my legs, but to make things worse, the dress barely reached my ass. Thankfully, they brought a bag of black shorts to wear underneath. I was very conscious of Rob, who kept looking my way, but I guessed I only noticed because I was having some eye trouble of my own. He wore a girly cut-off T-shirt. Mr. Abs. Things started to make sense. At one point, Vanessa caught me staring. I looked away quick, but my face got so hot and red, and it got even worse when I thought of Vinnie and how much I missed him. I felt pretty bad.

We went to the mall, which was a thirty minute drive. Mrs. Gallagher talked with security while we all floated around with our jackets on so as not to ruin the surprise. Finally, we were all told to linger around a covered courtyard area, where there was a gathering of people. Rob gave a great big wolf whistle that I was not ready for. My gut felt sick as I realized I would have to dance in front of so many strangers. My breathing got all weird, and I started feeling kind of woozy. I looked around for Kate because I knew to take my lead from her, but my vision wasn't working. I couldn't focus on anything.

Then the music started. By the time I saw Kate, she was already dancing in her group. I was supposed to be opposite. I pushed through the crowd trying to catch up. Then I realized I was still wearing my jacket. I threw it off mid-stride and struggled through all the strangers. At this point, the hip-hop dancers were throwing their shapes. The place seemed to be lit up with a light so white I couldn't focus my eyes. As I rushed to my position, hopping and skipping, trying to make it look like part of the act, it happened. Just as Rob went to lift and spin Vanessa, I accidently barged into him. They both came crashing down, hard, Vanessa almost landing on her head. They both howled. Vanessa got up, holding her wrist, and continued dancing. Rob tried to put weight on his foot, but he winced and sat back down. Then I looked up just in time to see Dominique trip over my jacket. She somehow managed to punch herself in the face as she tried to break her fall, and blood gushed from her lip.

Everyone stopped dancing, but the music still played.

I kneeled to check on Rob, and I could tell he was hurt bad. He was just shaking his head from side to side.

"Oh Jesus, are you OK? Are you OK?" I asked.

Vanessa came over and called me a stupid bitch just as the music was turned off mid-crescendo. The mall was completely silent except for a few volunteers, who shook their collection buckets.

I spotted Tammy and went straight over. "Let's get the heck out of here." But she just shook her head. These dumb security personnel came out of nowhere, and we had to stand around forever.

For the next forty-five minutes, we sat in a little room, waiting to get interviewed. Vanessa called her dad, and this tall, white-bearded man arrived soon after, his face angry. He examined her wrist and bandaged it up, then went to wait until we were done filing reports.

I hated having to share that tiny space with those witches who kept calling me a dumb redneck idiot. Rob refused to blame me, and he kept arguing with Vanessa. He called Dominique a stupid ditz. He even asked me in front of them if I was OK. I just kind of nodded. I was totally fine. This did not play well with Dominique and Vanessa. I wondered if I'd get in more trouble. Trouble loved me. But it was unrequited.

When we got home, I went in my room and didn't come out. At least Kate brought me the laptop, and I just watched movies to help pass the rest of the weekend.

Chapter 19

Sunday night, I was worried sick about going back to school, and just wanted to get the first few days out of the way.

At lunchtime, I decided to take a walk down by the football field. Even though the snow and ice had gone, the air remained crystal cold. Spring in Lakewood was sterile compared with the spring beauty we had in Kentucky. I tuned in to a couple of birds in conversation, but was soon interrupted by the sound of laughter. It was Donald and his gang of tenth-graders. They were headed behind the gymnasium, but Donald caught my eye and came over. Oh God, I thought. I did not want reminding of the incident.

"So, you wanna walk a little?"

"OK," I said, trying not to show my hesitancy. Then I immediately realized I didn't have anything to say to him. But it wasn't so bad. He was geekier than I had imagined, but kind of funny. He had a pet tarantula, which I thought was completely gross. I offered to kill it for him and told him I did a lot of stuff like that back home in Kentucky. The poor guy was trying his best to keep the conversation going, and he had no reason to, because it was a nice distraction. He kept fixing his thick-rimmed glasses, pushing them back up his nose.

"Quit it!" I said finally. "Here, give me." He didn't, so I tore them off his face and messed around with the arm, bent the metal a bit and handed them back. The guy had bluey-gray eyes, and man, you could tell he had the opposite of twenty-twenty vision. Without the specs, he was as good as dead round those parts. Poor guy looked so pathetic. I put them on his face and smiled.

We walked by Bailey, Dominique and Vanessa. Bailey stared at her phone, but Dominique licked her cut lip, and Vanessa looked like she wanted blood. My slightly better mood evaporated.

"Sheesh, those girls really don't like you, huh?"

"I guess not."

"I guess you know what girls are like. You guys get so jealous all the time, jealous of boys, jealous of each other. You girls can be so hateful."

After that, I didn't feel like talking to Donald anymore.

"OK," I said quickly, "I better go to class." I guess he figured he'd said too much, because his face kind of dropped, and he checked his watch. There was still fifteen minutes of break left.

"Yeah, yeah, me too, I guess." And he scurried away.

It was way too early to go to class, so I went to the bathroom, shut the door behind me, sat for a few minutes to gather my thoughts and breathe deeply. But really, I had chosen the worst place to get it together. A citrus- and urine-scented Zen was not what I had hoped for.

Just as I was washing my hands, the bathroom door opened, and in the mirror, I saw Vanessa and Dominique come in, malice painted on their faces. Vanessa crept quickly toward me. Dominique's dark eyes stood out like death against her pale cheeks. I backed away until I had nowhere to go. Before I could do anything, they grabbed an arm each and twisted them behind my back. The pain was so bad I felt like my elbows would snap. I tried to wriggle free and kick, but Vanessa punched me in the stomach. All the air left my lungs. My legs buckled, and I collapsed onto my knees. Dominique kept me restrained as Vanessa got up in my face and started bellowing.

"You little hoozie! We warned you to stay out of the way. You better crawl into a hole and die, or get lost back to your hillbilly yokel folk. Nobody wants you here."

"Look at my face, you freak!" Dominique spat.

Vanessa's bandaged arm didn't seem to be causing her much trouble. She saw that I had noticed, and next thing, she slapped me square across the cheek with her "sore" hand.

I tried to cry out, but Dominique tugged harder at my shoulders until the pain was unbearable. She clasped her hand over my mouth. I choked for breath as Vanessa produced something shiny from her jacket pocket. My heart thumped as blood streamed to my head. What was it? A knife? It was scissors. This was it. What were they going to do? Kill me? Cut me? They were going to cut my face so that I'd be a hideous monster for the rest of my life. Vanessa brought the scissors toward my throat. I closed my eyes tight and heard a loud snip noise. I waited for the pain. Just then, the bathroom door swung open, and Bailey came in. She called out, and Vanessa dropped the scissors. In the moment of confusion, I took my chance. I bit down hard on Dominique's hand. She released her grip, and I squirmed away and stood, lashing out at Vanessa at the same time. Dominique reached for me again, but I swiveled and kicked her in the leg, then pushed her with all my strength.

After that, I don't remember much except for pushing Bailey to the ground as I ran out the door. Some kind of logic made me stop running as I turned the corner, hoping no one noticed. There was blood splattered all over my shirt, and my hand was cut. I walked out the main entrance as normally as I could. I was miles from home and wanted to be anywhere but this hellhole. After a few minutes, the pain in my hand and face really kicked in. I was sad to feel so alive.

Chapter 20

I just kept walking and walking, directionless, one black shoe in front of the other, eyes dry — I refused to shed tears for those bitches — trying desperately to resist self-pity.

A song played in my head, rhythmic and fast, a mixture of the indie music I listened to mangled with Kate's Irish music. I let it carry me until I found myself outside the coffee shop around the block from home. I ventured in, pleased to see Nellie busy, taking orders. The doorbell jangled. She took an order, barked some instructions and then looked at me. Her eyes almost popped out of her head. She spoke briefly to a coworker and scuttled toward me. She was wearing glasses, which made her kind of geeky-looking.

"What the heck happened to you?" she asked, alarmed.

I shrugged. "Nothing," I said quietly.

"Nothing my ass! You have strangle marks on your throat, and your lip is busted. And … and look at your hand. Jesus! Oh no! Turn around."

She drew her fingers through my hair.

"Gosh, your gorgeous golden hair. Who did this to you? Oh no! Are you OK?" she asked, biting her finger.

I patted the back of my head and quickly understood. There was a huge chunk of hair missing, all the way to the scalp. Nellie rested her hand on my shoulder and stared at me with big, brown sympathy. I couldn't cope. A solitary tear splashed on the floor, and I was pretty sure the whole coffee shop heard. I had to work really hard to keep it together, and I guess Nellie realized that, because she ushered me under the counter and through to a back room. Another worker was sipping a frothy drink, feet up, reading a magazine.

"Hey, give us five, will ya?"

He took one look at me and scooted out of there.

Within minutes, Nellie had tied my hair in a bandana and was holding an ice pack to my face. I started talking, told her everything, having to stop myself from going too deep, going all the way back to the beginning, to Kentucky. It turned out Nellie knew of Vanessa. Her father was a big-time doctor at the Cleveland Clinic. He had left his wife, married again, and Vanessa had chosen to stay with him. Everyone has it tough, I thought. But still.

Nellie shepherded me back out to the shop and sat me down. She brought me over a book and then returned to work.

The book was *To Kill a Mockingbird*, which I had read before. I started into Scout's tales, and before I knew it, there was a steaming mug of hot chocolate on the table.

"God, Nellie, thanks. I don't know what to say."

"Never mind. Just enjoy it. Give yourself a break."

I took a sip, almost burned my tongue clean off, set it down and began to read, just picturing the kid's shenanigans as best I could. When I next thought to take a drink, it was almost cold, so I ended up downing it in one. I wiped my sleeve across my mouth, leaving a great brown stain. Tammy would kill me — even I would kill me for doing something so dumb. What did it matter?

Nellie wasn't around when I was leaving, so I just wrote a little note on a napkin, tore a page from a magazine and made her an origami boat. A lifeboat, I thought. I nodded to the manager as I left, and he winked as he wiped down the counter. A long time must have passed, because the light was getting low as I made my way home.

I spent another fifteen minutes outside, waiting for Tammy to finish up in the kitchen, wanting to go in unnoticed. I had a headache that was crying out for darkness.

There was a smell of warm pastry coming from the oven, but even that wasn't enough to stimulate my salivary glands. The sound of cartoons came from the living room, grizzly music from Bailey's room.

In the bedroom, I pulled the curtains, killed the lights and got under the covers fully clothed. I just wanted to wallow in my own misery. I found Kate's portable radio. I scrolled, skipping the chart garbage until I came to an oldies station. The songs were from the early 1900s and were really blue. I closed my eyes hard and listened to the words and the slow, sorry melodies. My eyes were dry, and my heart was like chalk, no more emotion. The only real feelings I had throbbed in my knuckles and around my neck. One slow, sad tune moved to the next, and even when jovial big-band songs played, I just felt numb.

The sharpness of the light woke me later, hurting my eyes. I took the ear buds out, ready to yell, but stopped when I saw Tammy. She came over and sat on the bed beside me.

"What's wrong, Alex? It's dinner time. I made roast pork in puff pastry. It's really good."

I just turned over and pulled the blanket over my head. "Go away," I mumbled.

"Oh, there's no need to be like that. Come on, we even got chocolate milk."

"I'm not hungry, Tammy!"

She got up and left, saying, "Well, if you change your mind," in her dumb Ohio accent. Anger replaced nothingness, and it took me a long time to fall back asleep. I didn't wake again until morning, and it was like déjà vu when Tammy turned the light on and sat on my bed once more.

"Come on, sleepy. You need to get up for school."

I groaned, could barely open my eyes. She put her warm hand on my forehead, and it felt good.

"Oh, you aren't doing so hot, kid. How do you feel?"

"Like ass," I replied in a throaty whisper.

"You know what, you just close your eyes, and I'll bring you some water and medicine, OK?"

I was glad I didn't have to go to school, and just slept and slept. I rolled over at ten-thirty when the phone rang. Immediately, I had a feeling of dread in my stomach, like something terrible had happened. I thought of Lucas, and my heart began to beat fast, my mind creating a new reality, one of a living hell on Earth. Tammy hung up, and she and the Old Buck whispered frenetically. My heart almost exploded when Tammy entered and pulled the curtains. I shot up.

"What is it? What is it?"

"I need you to get dressed immediately," said Tammy strictly. "Just like your mother!" Buck stood at the door, blank-faced.

"What's the matter?" I asked again. "Is it Mom?"

"No. Get dressed quick."

It didn't take a degree in anthropology to figure out what was going on.

"But Tammy, listen for a minute ..."

She picked up some laundry and spoke from a crouched position. "This is it, this time. I'm going to call your Great-Aunt Peggy in Virginia."

And she was gone. Old Buck stood in the doorway, staring not at my face but at my swollen hand and my neck. He took a step inside and cleared his throat. "Did you start it?" he asked softly.

My mouth opened, and I gurgled as words failed me. I gave one slow headshake instead. He looked into my eyes and left.

"No! NO!" I shouted.

Chapter 21

We passed Vanessa and a glammed-out, tall, blonde woman on our way to the principal's office. Vanessa's arm was tied up in a sling, and it looked like she had applied bruise-colored make-up to her cheek. I was surprised she wasn't wearing a neck brace. She just glared my way. I mouthed a swear word at her when I was sure no one was looking.

Tammy, Buck and I sat down opposite Dennaghy. His office smelled like leather, varnish and prejudice. All along the back wall hung photos of the previous principals, all suited-up and proud. There was a picture of his family on his desk—standard-issue wife and three young kids. He shuffled some papers and then cleared his throat.

"I'm going to get straight to the point. There's no easy way of saying this. Ms. Wallace's parents are filing two separate lawsuits, one against the school and one against your family, following this second incident."

"What?" I yelled. Tammy squeezed my leg.

"They are willing to drop the charges and the case against the school if we agree to expel Alexandra. The

Bielers and the Wallaces have been great friends of the school over the years, and all their children have passed through these corridors."

What in the heck was he talking about? I knew for a fact that Vanessa had only started school the previous year. It didn't take much figuring to realize what he meant was that Dr. Wallace had paid for the football field.

I was too outraged to take it all in. Neither Tammy nor Buck moved.

"And as you know, this is regrettable … Alexandra has shown a lot of promise in her studies, but behavior is paramount, and our school has a reputation to uphold. In life, there is no 'three strikes and you're out'. We've already had one incident and a suspension, not even three weeks ago."

His eyes darted from me to Tammy, then Buck.

"I'm sorry there's no other way to put it, but as of now, Alexandra's position in the school is untenable. As I said, you may also have to prepare for a legal case against the Wallaces. But if I may, I'd suggest an apology might …"

Lightening sparks flickered in my brain. He kept talking—with his suit and authority and total nonsense—just kept talking. Tammy and Old Schmuck just sat there and took it. And then I remembered. I was still wearing my bandana. I stood up, knocking the chair over behind me.

"This is absolute garbage!" I screamed. "Look at my neck. Look at the scratches on my face. Look at my hair!"

I whipped off my bandana, and three mouths fell open. "There were two of them and one of me. They attacked me the first time too. You didn't even ask for my side of the story. You're just a … I can't even say the words because God or Satan might strike me down. You are everything that is the matter with the world. You are part of the problem. You do what the money says. You listen to that! You are nothing but a … a … a freaking coward." I saw the fear in his eye and turned to Buck and Tammy, who were stupefied.

"I'll be in the car," I said, and walked toward the door.

"Just wait a second, Alexandra," Bucks said. I bowed my head and sighed. The leather chair groaned as he stood. My life was predetermined to be a minefield of shit. I trembled as a fist slammed the desk, rocking the entire room.

"You have some nerve calling us in here with these accusations, which are both unfounded and untrue."

I turned. Buck was livid.

"Our legal people will be in touch, Mr. Dennaghy. I don't think you or the Bielers or the Wallaces have their facts straight, as Alex rightly said." He paused. "If it looks like horse shit and smells like horse shit … well, you're a smart guy, you can figure out the rest. Come on, Tammy, let's go."

Dominique and her parents sat alongside the Wallaces in the waiting area as we left. I smiled and didn't so much walk as kind of groove, humming a little ditty, before turning and flipping them off. I felt invincible on my way back to the car. Tammy slammed the door behind as she got in.

"Just where on Earth are we going to get money for a lawyer? Hmm?"

I didn't care.

* * *

Tammy and Old Buck sat at the kitchen table for what seemed like hours. The place was a no-fly zone. My stomach rumbled. I hadn't eaten since the day before. Even Kate lay lifeless on the sofa. Finally, I was summoned to the table. Bailey, to my surprise, was also there.

"Sit, please," said Tammy as I stood awkwardly, my hands resting on the table's edge.

I was at one end, Bailey at the other, Tammy and Buck in between.

"We need to discuss everything that's been happening."

I heard a rustling at the hallway, and I guess Old Buck did too, because he took his wallet out of his pocket and fired it at the door. There was a startled yelp, and Buck roared. "Get back to the TV, Kate!"

Tammy continued.

"First of all, I want to apologize for not asking for your side of the story, Alex. For that, I'm sorry. I shouldn't have assumed." She paused for a second. Old Buck nodded to her in encouragement. "Now we need to know exactly what happened."

So I told them everything, even about the first fight, when I got suspended. I stared at Bailey with loathing eyes. I told them she had instigated it. She just stared back at me. Buck didn't speak, just used his ears and eyes, reading faces. Why would they believe me, after everything I had done?

"I reckon this talking makes no difference. Get me expelled—I don't care—and let me leave this hellhole and go back to Kentucky."

"You may get your wish, Alex, but we have the serious issue of a huge legal bill looming over us. Don't you understand?" There was fire in Tammy's eyes. Old Buck squeezed her hand.

"What the hell is Bailey doing here, anyway?"

Bailey looked away.

"She's here because she has also been suspended."

"What?"

"They found cigarettes and some other things in her locker. She claims they don't belong to her."

"Look, where are we going with this?" I asked, perplexed. "How can they sue you? They're the ones to blame. We should be suing them."

That's when the most unexpected thing happened. Bailey brushed hair out of her eyes. "Alex is innocent," she said.

"What?" Tammy and Buck gasped.

I was too astonished to respond. What was this? Some kind of sick joke?

"I know Alex is innocent."

I couldn't understand why Bailey would say this. She hated my guts. Part of me didn't want her defense. I was closer to home now than I had been in weeks.

"The girls had wanted me to do it, to warn her, to mark her, make her stop ruining our lives. But I couldn't."

I waited.

"Go on," said Tammy.

"They're my friends. They'll kill me. They'll ruin me." She started crying. Buck stretched his hand across. He was now holding both their hands, like it was a séance. Bailey gulped back tears.

"I walked into the girls' bathroom and saw them. Dominique was holding Alex. Vanessa had scissors."

Her voice was quivering, and I felt like getting violent with her. She was making herself out to be the victim.

"I guess they got startled when I came in. That's how Alex was able to get away and ... and ..." She started crying and then looked at me. "Just 'cause I'm sticking up for you doesn't mean I like you. I hate you. I hate you!" she yelled. She got up to run out of the kitchen, but Buck's booming voice caused her to step on the brakes.

"Get back here right now, Bailey. Apologize right now."

Bailey stared at the ground.

"Right NOW!"

"Sorry," she said. She said it a second time, and I guessed she only looked right at me because she knew Old Buck would probably have made her stand there until she did. Then she went to her room, leaving an eerie silence.

A triumphant silence.

Old Buck perked up. "OK, Tammy and I need to talk about this. Just because Bailey has said as much doesn't mean a thing. It's still their word against ours. Now go rest."

And I did. I rested.

Chapter 22

The following day, Bailey and I had to help Tammy with a complete spring cleaning of the house. We had to pack up winter and roll out spring. I almost didn't mind having to work so close to Bailey, knowing I had won. She was catty as hell, mumbling under her breath, huffing at every chore Tammy asked us to do, grunting every time her phone beeped. I just got on with the chores, finding the mindless tasks therapeutic.

After cleaning gunk from the corners of the windows, I got thirsty and made tea. I have no idea why, but I made two cups and left them on the coffee table. I sat and sipped mine for a couple of minutes and then got back to work. Bailey wiped a bead of sweat off her face. She saw the second cup, steam still rising.

"Is that mine?"

I shrugged my shoulders and continued working. After a bit, I heard her take several long drinks. I felt stupid and didn't want her to think I felt any gratitude toward her. After that, I cleaned mine and Kate's room.

Kate was acting weird when she got home from school. Whatever room I was in, she would sneak up and peak at me through a crack in the door and then run when I looked 'round. She even took to carrying a blue plastic baseball bat around with her, and hid behind one of Old Buck's hockey masks. Growing tired of her antics, I finally gave chase, Kate squealing like a warthog. I cornered her in Tammy's room. She cowered, both hands covering her face.

"What are you playing at, kid?" I yelled, and tried to pull the mask from her face.

"Let go of me! Go away! Go away!"

"Fine!" I huffed and went to leave, but only made it to the door.

"Are you a bad person?"

"What?" I snapped.

"Are you a bad person?" She was peeking through her fingers.

"Yes, I'm a very bad person, and I'm gonna be a whole lot worse unless you tell me what's going on?"

"Somebody said you killed a girl," she said in this little voice.

I couldn't help but laugh, a little snort first, then longer splutters. She looked back in surprise. Then I did a mwahahahaha-type laugh.

"You heard right, kid. I killed a girl, and you know what else? I ate her brains." I walked up close to Kate, pretended I was munching on a brain sandwich before tickling her head, but she just screamed God almighty and ran down the hall. I chased her, making chomping noises. She reached the bathroom and locked the door before I could stop her. I banged on the door. "I ate her brains because …"

There was silence. I made a few more nom-nom sounds and a little burp. Several seconds passed.

"Because why?"

I smiled. "Because eating brains makes me smarter."

More silence. "You're not going to eat my brains, are you?"

"I dunno, maybe. Now come on out of there, silly." The door opened slowly, and I gave her a hug.

"Please don't eat my brains. If you need to eat anyone's brains, eat Bailey's, OK?"

"OK." I nodded. "Now don't we have some dancing to practice? I need a change of scenery."

"I sure do, and you know, it's only ten days until the finals. I have so much to practice. But guess what?"

"What?"

"I got you a little present. Go out to the garage, and I'll get it." I stood, puzzled. She ran off, calling behind her. "Go on!"

I waited a couple minutes for her in the garage, and she came running in, her hands behind her back. She told me to close my eyes and put my hands out front, and when I opened them, there was a brown-paper parcel, badly wrapped, tied with gold string. She handed me a homemade card. It was just printer paper, folded down the middle. She had spelled my name Alexander, and the girl on front was like giraffe-Rapunzel with rivers of yellow hair. On the back, there was a picture of a kid dancing in a garden next to what looked like a giant watermelon, although it could have been a Christmas tree. I opened it. "To the best cousin eva!"

"You know it's spelled e-v-e-r, right?" Kate just grinned and nodded at the package. Her feet were all fidgety. She was more excited about this than I was.

"Open it. I tried to make a bow, but it was really, really hard."

I hated getting presents, and my heart kinda sank. Her face beamed up at mine, willing me to open it. I untied the cord, unfolded the paper bag and pulled out a worn pair of off-black heavy shoes.

"I know you wanted to try dancing in heavy shoes, so I got you a pair."

I was so happy I could have cried. I didn't know how to thank her. "But how? When? How?"

"It was easy-peasy. I saved up some of my pocket money for State and used that to buy them. They weren't much. Go on, try them!"

I unlaced my sneakers, sat on the floor and put them on. I tied them up and almost slipped as I tried to stand, throwing my hand out for support.

"Whoa!"

"You gotta be careful, Alex, or you'll break your neck."

"They're great! They fit real nice." I smiled, examining them. "How did you know? Were you measuring my feet while I slept or something?"

"No, dummy, I just checked the size of your sneakers one day. You're lucky you don't have to break them in. Normally we wear one size smaller."

I hugged her again. "God, thanks, Kate. You're an angel."

"OK, now dance, cowboy!" she said in a Western accent. She pretended to fire two pistols at my feet. She was definitely watching too many cartoons.

First off, I just tapped my feet and fooled around doing jazz hands. I slid across the floor making goofy Martin-esque sounds. I tried doing over-two-threes, but Kate told me there were different moves to learn for heavy-shoe dancing. All the same, I could feel right away how much harder it was than doing it in sneakers, how different it was from ballet, the extra weight making the moves feel clunky, harder to execute. With all the clattering noise, I wondered how they kept any timing at all. Kate's face glowed as I moved gingerly around the floor.

I felt the way she looked. In a matter of minutes, I was drenched in sweat, not from exertion, but from the excitement and buzz of dancing. It felt amazing. I messed around for another little while, both of us having fun, but I quickly remembered. There was only a week until Kate's competition, and this was about her. I stopped suddenly, turned and pointed a finger.

"Katie, this is the kindest thing anyone's ever done for me. Thank you so much. But we need to focus on you. Hurry up now and get your shoes on. We've got work to do."

We spent the next hour working on some of the things she had been having problems with—her high clicks and back clicks—making sure we heard all her rhythm. She was having a little trouble keeping her left foot turned out the whole time, so I helped her with that, offering encouragement, rewinding the music. She was so motivated. She was a winner, and there was no stopping her.

We finished, and Kate went inside. I sat on a chair, took off the shoes and held one up to examine it, admiring every weird-looking inch — the clunky heel and the wonderful soft, worn leather. The shoe was so floppy, yet Kate could still stand on the tips of her toes without hurting herself. They were just like a swollen tap shoe. I really loved wearing them, moving in them, despite how ridiculous they looked. The feelings of warmth and giddiness that had flowed through me as I goofed around with Kate returned. Perhaps my emotions were askew, exaggerated because of her kindness. Maybe it was because I knew that Kate going to State meant I was nearing the end of my time in Cleveland. Or maybe it was because I finally overcame the three bitches.

That night, I had a crazy dream. We were all in my house — Mom, Dad and Lucas, even Tammy, Buck and the girls, as well as Grandpa and Vinnie. The light was kind of soft red. Music played, I'm not sure what kind, but everyone was dancing, and everyone was smiling as they twirled and skipped and laughed. It was lovely. When I woke, I felt happier than I had in a long time.

Chapter 23

Something remarkable happened on Saturday morning. I was sauntering around the kitchen wearing a T-shirt and an old pair of Tammy's jogging pants as I made eggs for her. I had sent her back to bed, because she looked like she needed the rest. I only realized how ridiculous I looked when there was a knock on the door. I rolled up the tracksuit bottoms to make them look like shorts and found a damp sweatshirt in the linen closet. The knocking continued. Then I remembered the hole in my head and grabbed one of Old Buck's woolly hats. I looked like the world's biggest ass. Finally, I opened the door. It was Dennaghy, accompanied by Mr. Wallace. I felt foolish for making the effort.

"Yes?" I asked matter-of-factly. Dennaghy's mouth just dropped open. "Eh, can we speak to Tammy or John, please?"

"I'm afraid Tammy is unwell and can't come to the door. Is there anything I can help you with?" I gave my fakest smile.

They looked at one another and hesitated. Old Buck's truck swung into the driveway at that moment. He hopped out, fixing his pants.

"Everything OK here, Alex? These gentlemen giving you trouble?"

I felt so cool.

"Actually, Mr. Buckman, we were wondering if we could discuss something with you," said Mr. Dennaghy.

"I see. Will I need my lawyer present?" Buck smirked.

I waved them inside and pulled out a couple of chairs at the kitchen table, but nobody sat. Dennaghy looked at me, then at Buck and waited.

"I ain't going anywhere," I said.

Dennaghy fixed his tie and coughed into his fist. Mr. Wallace stared real hard at me, eyes ablaze. He was staring at my cut lip.

"We made some enquiries and talked with some students. Another girl has come forward with a complaint," said Mr. Dennaghy.

I raised my eyebrows. "About what?" I snarled. The kids here just didn't like me.

Mr. Wallace cleared his throat impatiently. "Let me just get to the point." His voice was like marmalade. "Vanessa, my daughter, has been … Well, she's been going through a hard time following the breakup of my marriage. She and my new wife … they don't always see through the same lens. Please accept my sincere apologies."

"Please?" I said. Old Buck came and stood by my side and squeezed my hand. Mr. Wallace took a step toward me.

"May I?" he asked, arm outstretched toward my head. I blinked. He carefully lifted the hat from my head and pulled my head toward him. I could hear him swallow. He handed me back the hat.

"I'm so terribly sorry, Alexandra." He looked at Buck. "We are in no way seeking to take legal action against you or your family, Mr. Buckman. It was the first I had heard of it when Mr. Dennaghy called me several nights ago. Vanessa has been misbehaving for months now and …" He nodded to Mr. Dennaghy, who took over.

"Bailey told me what really happened, on both occasions. It wasn't long before Dominique and her parents came forward. Dominique has since tried to distance herself. She blames Vanessa."

"Alexandra, my name is Dr. Wallace, but please call me Troy. I'm very sorry for the trouble and hurt we have caused you."

I just stood there dumb and mystified, rolling my thumbs. I knew he was speaking English, but it wasn't making sense to me.

Dennaghy broke in. "Alex, you are more than welcome to return to school immediately. We will help you catch up on any work you missed. You're a very bright student, Alex. One teacher described you as a pleasure to have in the classroom."

I smiled. "Ms. Jones?" I started feeling like queen of the world.

He nodded.

"Ha, I knew it. What about it, old-timer?" I said, and punched Buck's arm. I knew by now what shape his beard went when he smiled.

Dr. Wallace said, "I hope you aren't annoyed that I have this information, Alexandra, but I know your family is going through a hard time at present. I want you to know that if you ever need help with anything, absolutely anything, I will do whatever is in my power to help you."

He reached into his pocket and slid his business card across the table, but before I could pick it up, he pulled it back quickly, took a pen from his jacket pocket and scribbled on the back before placing it on the table once more.

"I am sorry for the trouble we have added to your already difficult circumstances." With that, he nodded to the principal, who pushed out his chair and stood. Dennaghy was blushing now.

"The school is very sorry about how matters were handled. There will be an internal investigation, and we will undertake to make sure such a thing never happens again. I wish your wife a quick recovery. Good day."

When the door closed, Buck and I just stared at each other. He was obviously as numb as I was. I picked up Dr. Wallace's card, which had his home and office numbers in bold writing above a picture of a waterfall. On the back, he had written his pager number and a little note. "Absolutely anything, anytime", it read. A surge of electricity passed through my body as my mouth formed a smile.

Finally, Old Buck spoke. "Well, I guess that settles it." And then I hugged Old Buck until I heard the air empty from his lungs.

Chapter 24

Saturday afternoon, I felt awesome. The thoughts of going back to school having gotten one over on both Vanessa and Mr. Dennaghy was just the best. But it didn't last long, as Tammy reminded me I had to go to the hairdresser. I didn't have many options when it came to disguising the gaping hole in my hair. One was to try to blend the rest in slightly as I waited for it to grow back. Another was to just wear a hat for the next hundred years. I was feeling bullish, though. The hairdresser handed me a magazine. I flicked through and found exactly what I wanted. I just pointed.

"Are you absolutely sure?" she asked.

"Do it."

But back at school, I wasn't so tough. I had just arrived when one kid yelled, "Hey, check it out. It's blonde Harry Potter. Except hot." It was really short. I looked like a boy, no question. In spite of that, word had spread about what had happened with Vanessa and Dominique. On my way to class at the beginning and end of every period, kids cried out, "Yo, Alex," all wanting to high-five me. Guys and girls. I. Felt. Awesome.

The week was crazy busy as I tried to catch up on schoolwork. I hardly got to see Kate because she had dance class with the other girls almost every night. I went with her on Thursday night. Everyone looked pumped. Aside from Martin, who was almost a guaranteed winner, Kate was their next best chance at getting on the podium, along with Lucy, a sixteen-year-old they thought might make the top ten.

I brought my heavy shoes so I could mess around a bit in a quiet corner and practice the one new move Kate had shown me. Soon I realized that had been a mistake. The damn shoes made so much noise. It felt like everyone was staring at me, the whole place silent except for my corner. My cheeks burned like wildfire.

I persisted and practiced with my back to everyone, but soon sweat started pouring down my brow. I was so embarrassed. I knelt and began untying the shoes, only for Martin to come sliding over with his goofy smile and huge cranium. His body would have a lot of catching up to do.

"Hello, princess."

"Go away!" I said firmly. His smile shrank. I shrugged. "Shouldn't you be practicing?"

"Ah sure, you know me, I can do those steps in my sleep."

His goofy smile matched his goofy accent. I knew I wasn't one to talk, but his was just ridiculous.

"You're having a wee bit of trouble with the trebles, aren't ya?"

"How the heck would you know that?"

"I've got big ears," he said, and wiggled them without touching. "And I can see it on your face."

I felt like punching him; it was the same line I had given Kate before.

He dragged me back a couple of steps, faced me and assumed the preparation pose. "Look here." He did the move real slow and then started talking manically, using his hands. "Don't worry about swapping feet just yet. Get it right on the right first. Go slow and get the feel of it. Close your eyes too, and listen to it."

I tried it a couple times with my eyes closed. When I opened them, Martin wore a half-smile on his face.

"Now, the left."

It was much harder on the left; I just couldn't wiggle it as good.

"Shake the left more. Feel it loose."

Eventually I could feel and hear that it sounded better.

"Aye, that's it there. You're startin' to find the rhythm with your left. Don't think too much about it. Just let the rhythm come naturally. Now try switching feet without stopping."

I tried my hardest not to look in the mirror to see if it was right. It felt pretty close. I was dripping in sweat.

"That's it. Keep practicing that. I'll be back over to ya in ten minutes. It's not bad. You're good—well, you might be, anyway, with a bit of luck. But you'd want to start skippin' and joggin', 'cause you're not fit enough for this business, princess." He laughed and ran off.

It felt good to know I was getting it right. I sat and sipped water and watched Kate do her final practice. Her whole demeanor had changed since the first time I had seen her in the old, dusty dancehall. She was calm and commanding. She danced like an angel in her light shoes and like a thunderous goddess in her heavies. I was proud of her, and told her so in the car.

"You know there's nothing going to stop you winning this, Katie."

"Thanks, Alex. I've worked hard, so maybe I'll get on the podium."

"Wow! You don't even sound excited or nervous."

"It's like that famous boxing guy said one time. The fight is won or lost in the gym, on the road, long before I dance under those lights."

Who was this kid?

"If only you could see me on Saturday. I'll be white like a ghost."

"What do you mean, if only? Why wouldn't I see you?"

"You mean you're coming?"

"Wouldn't miss it for the world."

Kate threw her arms around my waist.

Chapter 25

Friday was crazy busy. Kate stayed home "sick" because there was so much to organize, and with Tammy working late at the nursing home the previous few days, we were playing catch-up. There was this whole ordeal I could never have imagined. Kate had what she called a "list", but it read more like an epic novel. I learned a new word: bobby pin. There was so much to go through: getting fake tan done, fixing the wig, getting the dress ready by sticking on new diamantes, polishing shoes and buckles, making sure socks were whiter than snow. It was never-ending, and would have been really stressful were it not for what happened the past weekend.

I got home from school to find Kate up to no good. I said hi to her, and she clean ignored me, busy doing whatever she was doing. I took a closer look. She had poured a great big bowl of Cocoa Krispies and milk and was standing on a chair over the sink. She stirred and stirred the cereal before emptying the concoction into another bowl through a strainer.

"Jeez, Kate, what the heck are you doing?"

"Making chocolate milk."

"God, you know, I like chocolate milk too, but this … this is …"

"The other stuff isn't as nice."

"Ya reckon?"

She finally looked at me and headed toward the bin with a sieve full of soggy cereal. I dropped my mouth.

"Besides, I don't want to get fat from eating the crispies."

"No, no, no, no," I said, and rushed to stop her from dumping the food. "Getting fat? Who told you that? Won't the chocolate milk make you fat? Jesus, Kate, you're a kid, and you need all the energy you can get for tomorrow."

She pursed her lips before speaking. "Nicole said Krispies will make me fat."

"Nicole. Ugh. I'll show you fat." I pulled open the drawer, took out a spoon and shoveled the soggy breakfast into my mouth until it spilled down my chin.

Kate just giggled and dipped an empty cup into the bowl of freshly manufactured chocolate milk. She took a drink and walked off, milk dripping everywhere. "Whatever, fatty!" she called.

Not long after, I noticed a change in Kate. She was walking around practically naked, waiting for the fake tan on her legs to dry, and she looked oddly pale, in an orange sort of way. Then I saw Tammy's face. I wasn't imagining it. Tammy was totally anxious-looking, gray and worn out.

"What you got to be so worried about, Tammy? It's not you who's dancing."

She tried to smile as she continued sewing, but when she got up to get some tea, I saw her hold the side of her back and wince. Kate was distracted too, not her normal thousand-question self.

Bailey arrived later. She took one look at Tammy, made her some tea and told her to sit down. Bailey started getting dinner ready. Maybe she was sick too, with amnesia. She had forgotten she was normally a witch. I started helping out. We chopped and sliced in silence.

Just as I was setting the potatoes in the oven, I heard a scream from the living room. Bailey dropped her knife and ran. I burned my fingers on the dish before following Bailey. Tammy was slouched on the floor, barely conscious. Kate was holding her face, gasping.

"What happened? What happened?" Bailey whimpered as she got on her knees. Tammy's eyes were closed. Bailey slapped her gently on the face. "Mom? Mom?"

Then she checked for a pulse. I brought my ear to her mouth and could hear shallow breathing. Kate ran in with a wet towel and started dabbing it on Tammy's forehead.

"Quick, Kate, get Dad," Bailey shouted.

Kate sprang away. Moments later, Buck came running in.

"I'll call an ambulance," I shouted, and headed for the phone.

"No, don't," Buck said.

He lifted Tammy carefully. Her eyes flickered, and she tried to speak. Buck hushed her and nodded to Bailey. She went in front, opening the doors for Buck. Kate followed behind, stroking her mom's hair, crying gently as Buck rested Tammy in the back of his truck. I remembered when I had lain there semiconscious. Another rescue attempt. Old Buck barked instructions, and I tuned in once again. The keys. The keys to the truck were on the table. I sprinted. Bailey's face was covered in eyeliner. Kate had tears flooding down her face. Buck rolled down the window as he pulled out.

"Kids, go back inside. I'll call you soon."

"Hurry, Dad, hurry," Kate shouted, and the truck skidded away. Bailey sobbed quietly, and Kate sat on her legs in the driveway, crying loudly. The rain started to come down, but no one moved. Finally, I crouched beside Kate and pulled at her chin until she looked into my eyes. "Come on, Kate. We better go inside."

* * *

The fire purred as we sat and picked at our food in silence. When the phone rang, all three of us stood simultaneously, our chairs screeching. No one made a move to answer it; we just stood like meerkats.

Bailey finally spoke. "I'll get it."

I wanted to go outside, to not hear, not know. Why did things have to change? I swore under my breath. My eyes drifted to the ceiling, and I was close to getting up to go out for some air, but I forced myself to sit for Kate's sake. She made a move to go listen, but I caught her hand and pulled her close to me.

Bailey returned, her face paler than normal.

"She's in the hospital, and she's stable. They think she'll be OK, but they have to run some more tests."

Kate ran to Bailey and hugged her tight. I sat down and sipped my chocolate milk.

"We have to just sit tight for the next few days. Dad said he wants to stay with her for a couple of nights. He'll come back tomorrow to pick up a few things, and then he'll go back."

Kate put some potato in her mouth, but didn't chew. The food just rested in one of her cheeks, like a squirrel. Her eyes stood out from her face like the moon on a miserable day. We were all so still, lifeless. The kitchen too was silent but for the stew still bubbling on the stove. A smell of warm bread wafted from the oven. Kate swallowed carefully and put her fork down. It was just beaten to the table by the largest teardrop. Another one followed. She pinched the bridge of her nose and started to cry with measured control. She wiped her nose on a tissue.

"Hey, hey, everything's going to be just fine, Kate. You know that," said Bailey, reaching across to hold her hand.

And then I knew. I understood. And my heart wept. I couldn't look at the kid cry anymore; it was worse than being hit by a truck. It was worse than any pain. Bailey was still comforting Kate when I got up and walked to the hall door. I whispered Bailey's name. She just glared at me. I nodded for her to follow.

"I'll be back in a second, OK?" said Bailey.

I closed the living room door behind us, and we stood in the half-light.

"It's State Championships tomorrow. She can't go!"

"Oh, crap," said Bailey.

"Not good."

There was a long silence, and I choked on my words. "It's just not fair. This can't happen. She's been working on this all year. It's just not fair ..."

"We can't do anything about it."

"Can't we get one of the other moms to take her? What about Mrs. Gallagher?"

Bailey shook her head. "They'll have left tonight. They always stay overnight."

"Crap."

And then a light bulb went on in my head. "I'll take her."

"What are you, nuts? That's impossible!"

"It's not. We'll just take the bus."

"You're crazy, Alex. No way! First off, Cincinnati is hours away. You're fourteen!"

"Fifteen, actually." Bailey raised her eyebrows. "Come on, Bailey. Just because Tammy is in the hospital, does that mean we all gotta sit around and worry until she comes back just fine Monday morning? Kate has to do this."

"No, Alex. It's too dangerous. Besides, you don't have any money."

I nodded. My shoulders slumped, and I sighed. But I knew there was still a chance. "Yeah, it was just a crazy idea. It just kills me to see her like that. And don't tell me you don't know what this means to her."

Bailey paused for a moment. Then she snarled like a wildcat and walked off. I had started boiling up inside when she turned halfway down the hall and said, "Follow me." She unlocked her bedroom door, and I stepped into a small, cluttered room. It was like a nest. She pulled a little wooden box from under her bed. It had Josh's initials carved on the side.

"You should probably destroy that," I said as she rummaged around. She nodded blankly. Then she pulled out a bunch of folded ten-dollar bills.

"Take this," she said, her hand outstretched.

"Excuse me?"

"You're right. We have to do this for Kate. And Mom would have wanted this more than anything too. Let's figure this out, but don't say anything to Kate yet, in case ..."

I nodded and whispered thank you. Bailey may have smiled back; I couldn't be sure. I had never seen all her teeth before.

"There's one more thing I need you to do," I said, and I told her my plan. Her shoulders dropped, and she sighed, resigned.

"You are totally crazy!" Bailey said, and I followed her into the living room with the phone and shut the door. She dialed the number and cleared her throat before speaking with a slight Southern drawl. "Hello? Is that Dr. Wallace? Hi, this is Tammy Buckman."

I smiled.

Chapter 26

That Saturday morning, I woke at 5:10 a.m. I took a quick shower. Yawning, I brewed a pot of coffee and began making pancakes with the mix I had prepared the night before. When they were made, I set them on a tray in the oven and sipped my heavily sugared coffee for a moment. Kate groaned and turned over when I switched her lamp on, ready to lash out like a bear woken early from hibernation. I shushed her with a soft voice.

"Kate, Katie, wake up."

"Aw, Alex, go away. It's the middle of the night."

"Kate, wake up," I whispered again. Her nose wriggled.

"What's that smell?"

"Your favorite," I said. She rubbed her eyes and sat up, sort of happy, very much confused.

"What's going on?" she asked, her eyes still full of dreams.

"Shh! Just eat up, will you?" I said, putting the plate on her lap. "You're going to need all the strength and energy you can get if you're going to win this competition."

"What?" she asked, kinda angry, like she thought I was playing a trick on her. I squeezed my lips together, raised my eyebrows and nodded.

"You're kidding me, Alex. Don't kid. That ain't fair."

I pointed to the clock. "Come on. You need to be fed, dressed, washed and on the porch by 5:45."

"Ha ha! No way, Alex. You can't be serious."

"I am!"

Her face expanded to the point where I thought her skin would crack, and she lunged forward and hugged me. I scolded her with my eyes. "Hurry up!"

She saluted me like a soldier and began stuffing food into her mouth.

I went and poured a second cup of coffee and tried to eat, but couldn't. Then I double-checked my bag. Kate was soon ready, standing by the porch with her dance bag and dress bag before I'd drained the dregs of my coffee. It was a chilly dawn. Kate wanted to ask questions, but I told her not to worry, and we sat on the swing. At 5:50 a.m., a great white Mercedes pulled into the driveway. Kate's eyes went all gazumbo.

"Who is it, Alex?"

"Um, I guess it's a friend."

Just then, Bailey came running out in her nightie and kissed Kate on the cheek. "Good luck, little sis. You'll be great!"

She then looked at me. I just nodded. The driver got out, opened the trunk and took our bags.

"Thank you so much for doing this, Dr. Wallace," I said.

"No trouble at all, Alex," he replied, and opened the door to let us in. We sat back in the heated leather seats as the doors clicked shut and we zoomed off. We were both soon nodding off to the soothing sound of old jazz music.

Dr. Wallace drove us all the way to the Union Centre in Cincinnati and had us there at 9:15, almost two and a half hours before Kate's competition started, which was perfect. I thanked him. He had arranged for Lucy's mom to bring us back to Cleveland afterwards. Kate and I, despite our early rise, felt well rested. I had to pay to get in because I wasn't competing, and they gave me a wristband. Kate was incredibly relaxed, almost sedate, as we got in line to get her number card.

"I got number ninety-nine!" said Kate, suddenly bubbling to life.

"Ninety-nine? Jeez, how many kids are here?"

"A lot!" said Kate.

"Is ninety-nine good or bad? Do you dance last?"

"No. They pick the starting number out of a hat, so I don't know yet when I start, but I just love getting double numbers. Double numbers are my lucky numbers!"

Kate told me it was sometimes better to be one of the last to dance because sometimes judges would forget all about who they had seen at the start. She said some people said kids who danced first never scored as high as later kids because the judges needed to see a bunch of dancers before they knew what the standard was like and set a scoring benchmark. This confused me. If you were the best dancer, you should get 100, surely. That's how I saw it.

I was amazed at the venue they had chosen. It was a five-star hotel, and the competition was split between two enormous function rooms. I had literally never encountered so many people before in my life, and soon felt completely overwhelmed.

We held hands so as not to get separated from each other, mainly for my benefit. Somehow Kate knew the way, and I let her lead. We found Mrs. Gallagher and the rest of the dancers, including Martin, who was speeding around in his little black-and-green-trim shirt and slacks. He looked quite cute with his hair all gelled up. There was an older boy standing beside him, maybe an eleventh- or twelfth-grader, perhaps another dancer, although I hadn't seen him at class before. He wore jeans and a plaid shirt and didn't seem to be in any rush to get changed. The older kids obviously danced later in the day.

"Oh, there you are, Kate. About time," said Mrs. Gallagher, who then walked away all flustered. She gathered together her dancers from Kate's age group to get changed, and gave them a pep talk before they warmed up.

Martin came running over to me afterward, and asked me to show him the steps he had taught me. The older boy followed him. He rested his hands on Martin's shoulders and spoke with a soft Irish accent. "Is this lad giving you any trouble, is he?"

His smile was even more mischievous than Martin's. He had a glint in his eyes.

"No, he's fine. Don't worry." I looked from one Irishman to the other.

"Are you not dancing too?" he asked. I checked him out again. He was about an inch taller than me, with a mop of brown hair. He had freckles on his cheeks and nose and some stubble on his chin.

"No, not me, nuh-uh," I said. I took the two in carefully. "Ah, now it makes sense. You must be brothers. You're like a less hyper version of Martin, and your head is in proportion with your body!"

Martin whirled around, firing a fake machine gun.

"Aye, how did ya guess? It's not that obvious, is it? I'm Declan, by the way."

He offered me his hand, and I was just about to shake it when Martin crashed into a girl. They both fell over a bunch of bags and then struggled to their feet. Declan whistled at him.

"I guess the accent kinda gives it away. And, well, why do you keep asking questions twice in the same sentence, why hey?" I asked, mimicking him. The poor guy blushed. I guess he was trying to be friendly and didn't expect to get his ass busted.

Kate stood on my toe. "Ow!" I cried.

She looked at me, unimpressed, hands on hips.

"Alex? Seriously?" She grabbed my hand and pulled me toward the hall.

"OK, potato family, we need to roll on outta here," I said, and followed Kate to the warm-up area, still carrying her bag like she was the Queen of England.

"Do you like boys, Alex?" Kate asked as she maneuvered us through the crowd. I didn't get a chance to answer. "I think they're icky. One boy in my class has a girlfriend. He even takes her on dates. They go to the movies together, and to the park and stuff. I think it's just gross. And wrong. They've been together since kindergarten."

I didn't know how to respond.

There were so many people bumping into one another and chattering and breathing, and I started to wonder if there was enough air in Cincinnati to keep us all alive. I felt lightheaded. Had I looked in a mirror, I'm pretty sure my face would have resembled a fish. My stomach was also not so good.

This *feis* made the Columbus one look like a picnic. Kate pointed out some of the teachers from the other schools. They looked like they were in a separate competition, one to see who could wear the most ridiculous outfit. One guy with bleached hair was wearing a velvet waistcoat and jeans, his face red from screaming. Kate's little friend Sandra from before, came running over. They hugged.

"Oh my gosh, what number are you? I'm twenty-seven! It's the worst, it's just the worst!"

"Why?" said Kate.

"Cos they're starting at number nineteen!"

"I got ninety-nine," said Kate with a wry grin.

Sandra clapped her hand against her mouth.

"Why? What is it?"

"Oh my gosh, Kate, you'll never guess who's one hundred."

"Please don't tell me, please don't tell me," said Kate, both hands on her cheeks.

Sandra nodded. "Yep. And Nicole is ninety-eight, I think. Did you see her new dress? It's a Celtic Shine."

Kate was still in shock.

"What is it, Kate?" I asked.

"Samantha! I'm going to be on stage with Samantha! Well, I might be, if that's how the order comes up," she said with a whimper.

Before I got a chance to cheer Kate up, Sandra's scare-mongering continued. "It's just the most prettiest dress you could imagine, and she's wearing the new Shannon wig. She looks amazing, and the stage is supposed to be so slippery, like an ice rink, and —"

I twisted Sandra's lips closed and mouthed for her to shut up. Kate's eyes were all big and terrified. Sandra said a quick "see ya later" and scampered off. I had to act quickly before Kate's confidence plummeted.

First, I made her practice her steps and jump rope for a while to get her mind off things, but even that wasn't working out — her feet kept getting tangled in the rope. Other teachers shouted instructions nearby, and Kate's face was all anxious. She couldn't focus. Some girls giggled as they passed by, unmissable in their flamboyant dresses. I had an idea. I grabbed her hand and dragged her toward the foyer to have a look at all the different stalls.

"But, Alex, I need to get ready."

"Just for a minute," I said.

We had a look at all the sparkly crap: tiaras, shoe buckles, practice bags, magazines and the rest. It was probably like candy to Kate, who took ages examining the bags and practice gear. It seemed to calm her down a little, and when we continued with warm-up, she was a little more focused. Then it was time to go where the moms had set up camp. Kate went off with a couple of the moms and other kids to get her dress on.

Her face went back down to frown-town when she got back to me. Her dress was pretty dated compared to the others. Some kids, or I guess their moms, really had gone way over the top. Kate told me that some of the dresses cost as much as $3,000, and the likes of Samantha and Nicole got a new dress every year. It made me want to throw up. I wondered what I could do for my family with that kind of money. Kate looked so down. All the other girls had these crazy, fake, sparkly diamonds glued onto their socks and dresses. Kate had only a few. Her dress looked sad.

She pointed out Melanie and Kimberley and Siobhan and Susie, all girls from neighboring states who were champions in their own right. Some had won last year, some had done well at the Nationals, all apparently monstrously good. Kate started to droop.

"And see that girl over there—Clover? Her old teacher is one of the adjudicators. She's good, but she hasn't got a chance."

I followed her finger. "Clover? They called her Clover? Do they hate her or something?"

Kate just shrugged and lifted her knees to her chest. The fold-out chairs in the warm-up area were anything but comfortable.

"Some people say that judges favor certain girls and don't like others just because of what you wear."

"But, Kate, surely it's got nothing to do with how you look? It's all about the dancing, right?"

She shook her head sadly. "Not always, and sometimes the judges are friends with the teachers of the girls and show them favoritism like giving them a high score, and sometimes they put girls in the recall before they've even danced, and really they only notice the dancers that stand out because of the nice dresses. I heard some of the moms say a couple times."

"Well that's bu … baloney," I said. "But, Kate, your dancing is amazing. I don't care how good the other girls look, and honestly, I think they all look plain dumb. You're dancing rocks! You need to forget about all the other stuff and just go dance your heart out." When I realized that she was actually listening with her big dumb eyes, I kept going. "You need to feel the steps and let the music flow through you, let it warm you inside. So forget everything else. We didn't come here to win, but to enjoy it, because you worked hard for it, and we're just going to enjoy it and not think about winning or losing, for the most part. But we *are* going to win, you hear me?"

She stuck out a hand, and we high-fived and laughed. All the same, she looked a little pale. We both needed some air. I searched for the nearest exit and double-timed it outside.

The sun was big and yellow in the sky, warm enough so that people floated around without coats. Kids played on the grass beyond the flower beds and skipped and jumped along the steps to the entrance. We sat with our legs hanging over a wall.

"Hey, kid, are you hungry?"

Kate stared at a spot on the ground, glum, swinging her feet. Tons of people came and went, up and down the steps through the revolving door. It was easy to become transfixed. Some of the younger kids were having the time of their lives sliding down a marble banister. I dug my hand into my backpack and handed Kate a banana. She held on to it, her mind elsewhere. I snatched it back, peeled the skin and shoved it into her hand again. She attempted a smile.

"OK, kid, start talking," I said after she had successfully swallowed her first bite. "Does that taste good?"

She just nodded and forced her jaws to chew. "It tastes like honey."

I knew for a fact that it did not taste like honey, although there was an aroma of honey in the air.

"Hey, you know where honey comes from?" I asked.

"Flowers?"

"No, a bee's butt." She wanted to smile, but just couldn't. "Is it your tummy? You nervous? You feel like you're going to poop your pants? Lil baby need to go potty?"

She elbowed me in the stomach. Clearly humor wasn't the way forward.

"What is it? I can't help you unless you tell me." Nicole and her mom walked by, glowering. Kate's head sank to her chest. I puffed mine out with a big breath. "Is it Nicole? Or the other girls? You think they're better than you?"

Kate looked at me and spoke softly. "No. No, that's not it."

I checked my watch. "Well, what? What is it?" I was growing impatient. She needed to start thinking positive. I wasn't used to her being like this, and it was beginning to get on my nerves.

"It's Mom. I'm scared for Mom."

My face softened again as half a dimple hit me. I had to squint.

"Well, let me tell you this for certain. Your mom is totally fine—your dad said so himself. And you know what? By the time you wake up tomorrow, she'll probably be on her way home." Her face lit up just a little. "And you know your mom would love to be here watching you do what you love. You know she wouldn't be putting any pressure on you, just making sure everything is going like clockwork. She'll be happy with whatever place you come. If you come first or one-hundredth, she'll still be the same amount of proud, won't she?"

Kate nodded. "I guess."

"No guessing. Of course she would. You're already a winner in your mom and dad's eyes, and Bailey's. They want you to do what you love and enjoy it."

Kate smiled. There was a pause.

"But not me. I don't want to see your face ever again unless you win first place. Understood?" I looked at her as serious as I could for a long time before breaking into a smile. Her legs started swinging to a new beat, and she gave me a "yes, sir, Captain" salute.

Hanging baskets of colorful flowers drew my eyes and my nose—a wonderful vanilla fragrance that reminded me of the gorse bushes at my house, all yellow in summer. The place was pretty sweet. There was a winding, wooden staircase that led to plush rooms overlooking beautiful gardens, arrays of colors and flowers, water-fountain spraying gold into the sky. When I looked back at Kate, she had almost finished her second banana and was working her way through an apple and chugging juice.

"OK, kid, we better get you prepped. Let's go."

Chapter 27

The competition was running behind schedule, so we had some time before Kate had to dance. Back inside, she pointed out a middle-aged man with graying red hair. He was doing his best to go unnoticed, sitting sipping coffee, reading a newspaper, but people kept coming up to him, shaking his hand. Kate told me he was a dance director from one of the big dance shows, there to watch out for talented dancers in the senior men and senior ladies categories, although according to Kate, they often kept tabs on kids as young as fourteen when looking for future stars.

A giggle of girls passed by and smiled all fake at Kate. They were from a particular dance school in Illinois renowned for producing champions. In the past five years, their dancers had won major competitions in all age groups, and last year, they had five world title holders. The under-seventeens champion wasn't competing today, just supporting her little sister. I looked closely. She had everything—great clothes, gorgeous hair, wavy, cut to her shoulders. She was tall and slim like a model. She came toward us.

"Oh, hey, your number's kinda falling off. Here, let me fix it," she said, and knelt to the dusty floor.

"Thanks!" beamed Kate. I swore to myself. How had I let that happen?

"No worries, number ninety-nine. What's your name?

"Kate."

"I saw you warming up, Kate. You have great feet. Hopefully I'll get to see you dance. Good luck."

She dusted the dirt from her black jeans, smiled at me and walked away. I hated her. Who did she think she was? Kate couldn't stop smiling.

"Did you hear that? Maura said I had great elevation. That's awesome! Maybe I should go get her autograph."

"Maura? Autograph? What are you, nuts? She's like sixteen. Who gets a sixteen-year-old's autograph?"

"She's seventeen," said Kate, a stern expression on her face. "And she's the best ever. Even Bailey says so."

I looked around. One guy was making elaborate hand gestures as he told some women a story. There was a pen sticking out from behind his ear, so I grabbed it. "Here, go get a piece of paper. I'll give you a freakin' autograph."

He looked around and caught me. I just smiled with all my teeth and handed it back. "You dropped your pen, mister."

"And when she finishes her exams, she's going on tour with a big show in Europe. Can you imagine that? Seeing all the places in the world, all from doing a job you love. That would be the best thing that could ever happen, wouldn't it?" Kate's little face was in overdrive, her eyes in a far-away place.

I sighed. "Listen, Katie, sure that would be great, I guess, but we need to focus on now, getting ready to dance. We can't think too far ahead. Just focus on doing your best today and enjoying yourself, OK?"

She agreed and offered me another captain salute.

"Quit doing that!"

On our way to the hall, we passed a magazine stand. A photographer took pictures of Nicole while another lady asked her questions. Kate told me rather bluntly that Nicole had been chosen for a feature in *Dare to Dream* dance magazine. Kate kicked an empty water bottle out of her way as we passed. I smiled.

We had to stand in the hall because side stage was reserved for the first crop of dancers. The under-seventeens champion, Maura, was there making nice with an older man and sipping a coffee. I didn't know what I wanted more, the coffee or to have her life. She seemed so at ease, carefree, confident, while I was an anxious wreck with no idea where my future would take me. I had to concentrate hard to bring my mind back to the dancehall, to Kate, to the noise. Maura came over again.

"Hey, ninety-nine. You know, they're just about to start. Shouldn't you get your wig on?"

Kate looked at me like it was Armageddon.

"What is it? What's up?" I asked.

"I gotta get my wig on, but Mom's not here to do it."

"It's OK, I'll help," I said, but she just started shaking her head.

"Nuh-uh, you won't be able, Alex. Oh no, what am I gonna do?" she cried, looking around for a genie.

"Don't worry, I'll help you. Come on. Where's it at?" asked Maura.

I tried to incinerate her with my eyes.

"Really? For real?" asked Kate.

Maura stretched out her hand. Kate grabbed it, and they ran toward the moms who were minding the bags in the warm-up area.

Twenty minutes later, Maura delivered the kid back to me, wig in place. I thanked her though my teeth. We went to the marley floor in the practice area, and Kate tapped and fidgeted her heavy shoes. I was glad of the padded floor.

"Don't worry, kiddo. You are confident. You've worked hard."

But Kate had a new expression of fear on her face. "No, look. It's number ninety-seven. I might be going on stage with her."

I looked over my shoulder. A pretty girl with a sour expression stood tall, stretching out her legs. "Who? Lemon Face?"

Kate nodded.

"So?"

"So? She won this competition last year!"

"You're on with last year's winner and Nicole or Samantha?" I immediately regretted my words.

"Maybe," said Kate, her little face full of fear.

"But you're gonna win it this year, so big schizzle!"

"No, Alex, the judges will only be looking at her. That's the way it works. Remember? They only watch people they know won before."

"Well, give them something to change their minds," I said with a wink.

Kate kept practicing, but she was getting real flustered, and at one point, actually kicked her shinbone when she tried some move or other. You could tell she was in pain, but she just kept on doing a certain section of a dance. I knew she was about to start crying. Finally, I grabbed her shoulders and forced her to stop. She was breathing hard, lips forced shut, eyebrows in a V-shape, trying not to lose it.

"What is it, Kate? What's going on?"

"I can't do it, Alex. I can't remember my steps. My head's gone all fuzzy."

"But Kate, of course you can. Come on, girl, we've done this like a million times."

A tear tricked down her cheek. Numbers seventy to one hundred were then called side stage, and I looked around as there was a miniature evacuation from the practice area. Kate looked like she was holding back the tears. I exhaled, my own mind whirling, and made her stand aside, taking her spot. I closed my eyes and quietly hummed the hornpipe beat, trying to visualize what we had done in the garage.

"OK, it's something like this." And I did my best to recreate what I could see in my mind's eye, just hoping it would spark her memory. "Is this working? Is it doing anything?"

"I think so," she said, nodding her head weakly.

"C'mon, you'd better go."

Kate gave me a quick hug and rushed off. She looked back at me. "Wish me luck?"

"You don't need it!"

I went down to the back of the auditorium, where some of the moms were, and sat. Number eighty-four stood on stage in preparation mode, and all of a sudden, got sick everywhere. I knew exactly how that kid felt. I almost didn't want to watch.

Finally, it came to Kate's group. Whatever way the numbers fell, Kate ended up being in a trio with last year's champion and Nicole, but not Samantha. Lemon Face and Nicole strutted onto the stage like it was some kind of dancing Barbie catwalk. Their shoulders were almost touching their butts, such was the arch in their backs.

Kate lined up on Nicole's left, farthest away from me. She looked completely petrified. The keyboard music began, and my heart started palpitating. Just as we came to the end of the eight bars of introductory music, Kate closed her eyes. She started dancing with her eyes still closed. But I was getting distracted. Sitting right in front of me was Nicole's mom and a large group of idiots who kept bopping and standing in my way. I clambered toward the aisle, craning my neck to see Kate's dancing as best as I could, and rested against a wall closer to the stage. Before long, she was zipping around and doing her moves over by my side of the stage. She had unbelievable presence and danced with such power, the moves executed with precision, her smile illuminating the hall. Everything just went perfectly with the music. She did one of my favorite things—walking on the blocks of her feet—quickly followed by a wobbly ankle trick and a karate-chop click right above her ears. It looked great.

I tried to keep an eye on how Nicole and the other girl danced. They both seemed pretty good, although Nicole and the third girl fought for the judge's attention, stage center. It was hard to take it all in, and couldn't have been easy for the judges either, but I guessed Kate was right about the dress. Nicole's embroidered black and silver dress shimmered, whereas Kate's looked like it had been passed on by a generation of homeless jig girls.

I felt so proud as the dance came to an end. Even though I didn't know much, I thought Kate's performance was much sharper than the other two. I just hoped the judges thought the same. With a bow and a pretty, genuine smile, she was gone, and Samantha and another girl took her place. Then I realized I was standing directly next to Dominique. She stared at me with a blank face. Mine was still delirious from watching Kate.

Dominique's beady black eyes kinda softened, and she spoke. "Kate was really good," she said, kind of hushed, and then left.

I didn't have time to process it all, because soon Kate was by my side, panting. She took the water bottle from my hand without acknowledging me and fixed her eyes on Samantha's dancing, catching the last few bars. I couldn't tell whether she was really good or the other girl was really bad. The other girl was real tall for her age and seemed kinda crooked when she danced and definitely not in time with the music; even I could tell. When they were done, Kate turned to me. I felt like such an idiot, but couldn't help glowing.

"Kate, you rocked it, dude."

"Thanks," she said, still catching her breath. "I think I did it good. I might have missed a back click, but I can't even remember."

"Did you enjoy it?"

"Yeah, it was great. I felt awesome. After the first few bars, I didn't even notice all the people or the lights."

"And what about Samantha?" I asked, peeling an orange as we plowed our way outside.

"Yeah, she did a good dance. It was pretty good," she said, nodding, neither happy nor worried.

I took that as a positive and handed her the dripping orange.

There was a break for the under-nines as the competition continued with a younger age group. It was incredible, really—so many kids and categories. It sure was a major operation and a hell of a long day.

First, we ate a snack, and then went for a stroll around the gardens and just chilled out on the steps until it was time for the next round. Kate went to the bathroom, and I waited for her in the warm-up area. I was waiting ages for her to get back, and started getting worried that something was wrong. I went looking for her, but it turned out there was just a huge line for the bathroom. She quickly changed into her light shoes.

"OK, I reckon the reel is next?"

"Yeah, you're getting it."

"Listen, kiddo, that reminds me: if you get lost and don't get on stage, does that mean I have to dance for you?"

She burst out laughing.

"Hey! What's so funny about that? You think I'm terrible, don't you?" I said, insulted.

"Well, you kinda are!" she said, sticking her tongue out. "Well, you're not terrible. You're good, but you just don't know all the moves yet. I wasn't laughing at you; I was picturing you all big and goofy dancing alongside the little girls. It would look funny!"

I smiled. "OK, so here's a new rule: if anything happens, like we get separated for a long time, I want you to wait for me at the vending machine in the foyer, OK?"

"OK, but what if you don't come to the vending machine and some other person comes and says something like 'your cousin is looking for you' and I believe her, and then I follow her, but she just puts me in the back of her car and kidnaps me?"

The whites of her eyes were enormous. "Ugh, Katie, that won't happen. Tell you what—we can have a code word in case I get held up for some reason and can't come get you myself."

"OK, sure. Sounds good to me."

We walked toward the warm-up area in silence, and Kate glanced at me.

"Hey, Alex?"

"Uh-huh?"

"What's a code word?"

"Ugh … a special word that only you and I know … like … Buttons? If the person says Buttons when you ask them what the special word is, then you'll know to trust that person, OK?"

She planted her butt on the ground and retied her light shoes. I had a feeling it was still not OK.

"But what if the man comes and I ask him for the code word and he says Buttons, but it was just a lucky guess? What then, Alex?"

"Ugh! Well I guess that's just bad luck for you then, isn't it?"

Kate's eyes opened wide, but I just stuck my tongue out. "Hurry up and tie your shoes, will you?"

Kate started complaining about how hot and heavy the wig was.

"You know what? If I danced, I'd refuse to wear the damn thing. Man, if you want to stand out from the rest, that would be the smartest thing to do."

Chapter 28

Kate stretched some more and then practiced her steps in the warm-up area before going side stage. I went back into the hall. I got to see a lot of the other kids dance, which was kind of interesting. At times, I had to try real hard not to laugh out loud. Maybe I didn't know a huge amount about Irish dancing, but I had learned enough to know what not to do.

The concentration was too much for some of the girls. Despite the intricate moves, some of the girls had real trouble keeping their arms by their sides. Some flailed their arms so much it looked like they were waving "Pick me!" to the judges. Smiling was also an issue. A few girls were trying so hard to smile that they actually looked like they were wearing Scream masks. Some had their chins too far back, as though their wig was made of lead. Others had their chins really far forward. At one point, I was clenching so hard, hoping a drop of pee wouldn't come out. Coincidentally, it wasn't just me who had trouble in that department. There was a hold-up when a girl peed in her dress right on stage, just before her dance was supposed to begin. She started crying. The dude with the mop was earning his money. It was kinda funny, kinda gross, but mostly terrifying.

Kate's turn came 'round, and she got up on stage once more with the same girls. She didn't seem worried about being beside two champions. But Kate was too innocent. Nicole seemed like the envious type.

Kate lined up to the left of Nicole just as before. She looked a little pale as the light beamed into her poor little eyes.

Then Kate closed her eyes and took off with the rhythm, from composure and focus to graceful power. She was over and across the stage, executing everything to perfection, as far as I could tell, anyway. I found my foot tapping to the music. She was so light on her feet, leaping and almost hovering in slow motion, all the while keeping perfect time. She was able to dance real high on her toes, and I don't know how she didn't break her ankles when she did the over and back wriggle on her tiptoes.

The other girls seemed to dance well too, particularly Nicole. I bit my lip. I kept my eyes open for the fancy footwork bits Kate had been working on in the garage, and she seemed to nail it on both feet, almost without thought. She bobbed across the stage like a bird, perfect in her beautiful, dimpled way. If only Tammy could see her. She bowed, and I waited a while for her to come back to my side.

"That was just awesome," I said. "I wish I could dance like you."

"You will, Alex, someday. It felt good. I felt like I was just floating out there, like I wasn't even in my body, like I was whisking around like … like a … like an out-of-control whisk."

Kate explained to me that the judges would choose the top thirty or forty kids, who would be recalled to dance a final round. I decided it was an ideal time to refuel the dance machine, just in case.

I used some of Bailey's money to buy lunch, and we sat and ate in the crowded coffee shop. I sipped gratefully on my large coffee. Martin's big brother caught my eye as he walked back from the line, and he diverted toward us a little keenly, almost tripping over an older lady. I worked hard not to laugh as his poor face went blister-red, but soon the urge to laugh had disappeared.

"They're announcing the under-nine recalls now," he said.

"Already?"

Kate started stuffing her sandwich down her throat.

"Stop, Katie. Just bring it with you." I got up and stared sadly at my mug of coffee.

"Do you want me to mind that for you? Youse will only be gone a few minutes," said Declan.

I nodded and left, forgetting my manners.

The room was totally hushed, and we had to tiptoe in and stand down back. Kate seemed totally calm; I wished I felt the same. An announcer stood on stage, fiddling with a microphone, a piece of paper waving loosely in his other hand. Finally, he called out numbers.

Kate and I hugged as the first numbers were read. Then we separated and focused, eyes like laser beams.

There was some general applause for the first few numbers. I started to get really worried after the first ten were called and Kate's wasn't among them. I held her hand, which was neither clammy nor dry. The next ten numbers were called; girls near us hugged and cheered. One girl started boogieing, an obnoxious grin on her face. Then came Nicole's number. Her mom jumped around like an animal that had just been shot in the ass. Dominique lifted Nicole high into the air, swinging her around, knocking into people without a care. I gritted my teeth and shot them a look. All the while, Kate was still composed and relaxed.

And then the announcer said "Number one hundred" and smiled and walked off stage. My heart just plain plummeted. I racked my brains for something to say, some way to console Kate. I started thinking about the ride back to Cleveland with somebody else's mom, how miserable it would be, Kate sad and worried sick about Tammy. I couldn't even breathe, just closed my eyes and thought about how terrible life was. I thought about Mom, Dad, Lucas, how messed up my life was. I must have been in a daze, because when I snapped out of it, Kate was saying my name as a final round of applause went up.

"Alex, it's OK. You can open your eyes now."

"Oh God, I'm so sorry, Katie. You were amazing, you know that? Don't be sad."

"It's OK, Alex, I know."

I rambled on until Kate put her index finger on my lips. My heart tried to pick itself up off the floor.

"C'mon, I need to get my hard shoes on."

"But he didn't call your number."

"Yeah, he did. You just couldn't hear it good because of Nicole's dumb mom, but he said it straight after. Number ninety-nine. I saw his mouth say it."

"Holy cow, Katie! You did it!" I hugged her hard, and then composed myself. "I mean, of course you did. OK, let's go!"

Chapter 29

Because of how it worked out, Kate was the second last to dance. Her final dance was a set dance that Martin had taught her. When she told me this, I nearly freaked out.

I left Kate to go backstage and went inside the hall to wait. At this point, I got confused. An announcer called out the most bizarre names before the girls danced: "Number seventy-four, dancing *The Three Sea Captains*". The ridiculous names continued: *The Drunken Rambler, Walk the Planxty*. They helped ease the tension in my shoulders, even if it was just temporary.

Kate's turn came. She stood on stage, her body relaxed but rigid, all by herself this time. There was no one to bump into her, distract her or knock confidence. Each of the three judges had their eyes firmly on her ratty dress, her sweet smile and her amazing feet.

She closed her eyes a second, and when she opened them, she had a transfixed look on her face. She took flight, her feet dancing light-speed, ferocious and precise. It was so skillful and quite beautiful. I could never have imagined myself thinking that, but I couldn't deny it. It was a dance I had never seen before, a series of fancy tricks, one after another. She had never practiced this with me in the garage. Everyone in the hall watched with sticky eyes. With each surprise, another mouth dropped open. I felt so fuzzy and excited inside.

Everything was faster. Kate trebled and moved into an axel spin, then lightning fast across the stage, in the air clicking her heels, sharp like calligraphy. It was mesmerizing. The two minutes passed, and I don't think I or anyone else dusted a molecule from their eyes. Despite the audience having watched a million dancers all day, there seemed to be a significantly louder round of applause than usual as Kate took her bow. I was flushed with excitement.

I couldn't be sure, but the auditorium felt weird, like time had changed color, like we could see the air we breathed. But the judges just rang a little bell signaling the next dancer to get ready. One guy cleaned his glasses and then marked his card; the others did the same. Samantha stood side stage. I caught a glimpse of the seventeen-year-old champion, Maura. She seemed kind of stunned. I cursed myself for not knowing more about the dances, about the techniques. Sure, I knew it looked amazing, but I had no idea how hopeful I should be. It didn't matter, I reminded myself quickly.

"Katie, that was incredible! Well done," I said as she approached, my hand held in the air. She smacked it really hard and guzzled some orangeade, not saying anything, her nostrils flaring. I could tell she was pleased. She took a bite of a chocolate bar.

We watched the last part of Samantha's dance. She got a huge round of applause too.

Mrs. Gallagher ran over and hugged Kate. "I'm so pleased, Kate," she said. "That was the best I've ever seen you dance."

Kate spotted some friends and asked me if she could go outside and play. We went and got her changed out of her dress real quick, and then she ran off. She was a baby tiger, full of playful strength, keen to explore and discover. She didn't seem worried about Tammy or the results. I wished I were more like her. But maybe dance and play were how she distracted herself.

Even though all the dancing was over, my anxiety levels were high. The hall had emptied out a little, so I closed my eyes and tried to regulate my breathing. I thought about the truck ride to Ohio all those weeks ago. I was so close to home, not just in proximity, but in terms of time too. I pined for Mom, Dad and Lucas. I thought about Harper chasing his tail, Vinnie chasing mine. Everything whirled, blurry images of a life I had before. It almost didn't seem real. If I didn't get home soon …

The images became vivid: a cloud, a great white cloud, a wooden house alone in a field, a red ball caught in the branches, the horse, feisty from winter, let loose and bucking blue murder.

I jumped with a start and whipped my head 'round, searching for Kate. I needed another coffee real bad. I remembered poor Declan and scurried out, hoping he wasn't still waiting, holding our table.

Kate was outside by the fountain with a bunch of kids. The foyer was packed with nervous moms and teachers smoking, their chatter short and excited. Someone nudged my elbow as I walked over to Kate. It was Declan. He handed me my coffee cup from earlier. I blushed. He wished Kate good luck. They were getting ready to leave. He was flying back to Ireland on his own later that evening. In his dumb accent, he said, "Ack, sure, you never know, we might bump into each other again."

The kid was weird, just like his brother. But nice all the same.

Martin had abandoned his winner's trophy and was chasing a bunch of girls around. He came over and told his mom he wasn't ready to go.

"Why not?" she asked. "Having too much fun? Gonna miss your girlfriend?" She winked at me. Everyone laughed except Martin.

"No, I want to see Kate win. Please, Mammy, can we wait a while? It won't take that long. Please?"

And then he was gone again, chasing Kate and the other girls, making motorbike noises, changing invisible gears.

People began to make their way back into the hall, and we followed, hoping to grab a seat before the results were called. Kate walked by my side. Her face was kinda icky and sweaty from playing.

Before we went into the hall, I heard a high-pitched yell. I turned 'round, and there was a lady in red pointing at me, two security guards by her side. I recognized her immediately. That silver-black hair. She was the bat-shit-crazy mom I had seen at Kate's dance class a couple times. She was drinking something out of a child's sippy cup. I don't even think she had a kid who attended dance class.

"That's the girl there," she said pointing. "She took little Kate without her parents' permission. I called their home and spoke with her father. He was worried sick."

Oh boy, I thought to myself. "What are you talking about?" I yelled.

"You told one of the mothers that Tammy would be along shortly. Where is she, then? I've heard about you, young lady. You're nothing but bad news."

Kate held my hand tight and looked up with big white eyes.

"I ... I ... Tammy is out in the car."

"Young lady, you are telling lies. Tammy is back in Cleveland, in the hospital."

Declan slowed down as he passed on his way to the hall.

"You two girls better come with us," said one of the security guards.

"NO!" shouted Kate. "The results are being announced right now."

The security guard grabbed Kate by the arm, and she started screaming. "No! Get away from me!" He took a firmer grip, and she screamed again. Then she looked up at me. "Alex? Make him stop."

"Leave her alone!" I shoved the guard as Kate tried to wriggle away, and he held on tight. A second guard came forward and quickly locked my arm behind my back. I squealed in agony. I tried to break free from his grip, but I soon gave up, the pain unbearable. Then I unleashed a volley of foul language at him. As they dragged us away, Kate began to cry hysterically. I felt like screaming the house down. They wanted to take us to the hotel's security center. I threw myself onto the floor. He would have to cuff me and carry me before I'd allow that to happen.

Then there was another shout.

"Wait! Wait just a minute." It was Mrs. Gallagher, moving faster than she had in thirty years, probably. We waited what seemed like an eternity for her to catch up, and by the time she had regained her breath, I had pretty much figured out what she would say.

"These two girls are with me, so let them go immediately. Kate's results are being announced, and Alex has to get changed to dance shortly after. Here."

She showed the guards her I.D., and they nodded to one another.

"Sheila, you'd do just as well to keep your nose clean out of things sometimes," she said to the lady in yellow who had ratted us out. "Come on, girls."

Mrs. Gallagher hurried off with Kate to get her changed back into her dress. I ran into the hall, and all I could see was a huge screen and nothing but tons and tons of numbers. I had no idea what was going on; there was an overload of information my brain couldn't process. Everyone was whispering and mumbling. It was like the Queen Bee's wedding day, live from the hive.

Eventually, I was able to figure out a certain amount. A column on the left-hand side contained the numbers of the thirty or so contestants who had been recalled. To the right were the scores of the three judges. The points didn't seem to get called out in any order that I could make out. It was just dozens and dozens of digits. The first two rows of judges' results had been added to the board, and the third were in the process of being announced. But there was no total, so it was impossible to see who was winning. I guessed people were just adding up their own scores before trying to work out who was in the lead.

Kate's scores were down at the bottom of the grid. I tried to add them, but there was no way my brain was going to do the math; my mind was just in too much of a whirl. Some people nearby cheered loudly. Dominique's normally pale face was all flushed as she gripped Nicole's hand. Kate came panting into the hall, checking the screen for a moment. She fidgeted. The whites of her eyes were as large as the heavens, the smallest tear stuck to a clump of mascara.

She kept looking at me as the numbers were called. "I'm not going to make the podium, am I?"

I nearly laughed at the bizarreness of her words. My eyes welled up so bad that I started to cry. I didn't have any words to make everything better. Here was a young girl who had dedicated everything to winning this one competition, and she wasn't going to be rewarded. And for what reason? I got angry. Because of the costume? Because of me? Because of the time when I had pushed Nicole at the Columbus *feis*?

Kate started twitching like crazy, puffing air. Another girl in a pink dress who had caught my eye earlier started cheering with her family. Finally, the grid was complete as the last of the judges' scores were entered.

The hall fell totally silent. Kate started crying, and I guessed she hadn't even finished in the top ten. Samantha was also crying and hugging her mom. My eyes immediately darted toward Dominique and Nicole.

Suddenly it made sense, and I screamed. Martin came out of nowhere and grabbed Kate. Mrs. Gallagher came and lifted her into the air. Declan came over to me with a scrap of paper. On it, he had written Kate, Samantha, Lemon Face, and Nicole's totals. The points flashed on screen. The final judge had given Kate 100. She had won by five points.

"In first place, number ninety-nine."

Kate, the clickety-clack usurper, came running over and leapt into my arms. We both cried tears of absolute happiness. I swung her 'round and 'round until I remembered. "Go quick, Katie Kat. They're waiting for you."

There was a short delay as they lined up in order side stage, but soon she was shaking hands, wiping her eyes with the back of her hand, her face all teeth and crater on stage. Kate stepped onto the number one spot and waved and smiled and cried and laughed. And I cried too. I wished I could have taken photos of her receiving the cup, but it was so big you couldn't see her when she held it anyway.

"Ladies and gentlemen, in first place: number ninety-nine, Kate Buckman," said the announcer, all loud and cheery. Her name appeared on the screen, and I felt so warm. A mash-up of a pop song and some Irish music started playing, and the kids boogied on stage. Mrs. Gallagher took some photos with her iPhone.

I went right up front to wave and cheer for her. Some people didn't look too happy that the three favorites had been beaten, but so many others clapped and cheered. They knew Kate was a deserving winner. Only later did I realize, had she been old enough to compete at Worlds, she would theoretically be the champion.

All the other kids wanted to congratulate Kate, and it took her ages to get back to me. She handed me the cup, barely able to speak.

"I'm so proud of you! Wait till Tammy hears about this, and your dad and Bailey. You're a legend, kid! You're going to be the winner for years to come, sweetheart."

Just when I thought the whole thing was done, Kate told me the winners from each age group came on stage together to dance again. She changed into her soft shoes and ran off to join the others.

The winners lined up, and one by one, they showed off to the audience as winners. They were allowed to dance to a few bars of music and enjoy the crowd's applause. The Parade of Champions, they called it.

Finally, it was Kate's turn. She had a new smile, one I hadn't seen before, as she danced. She was almost better than before, relaxed and really enjoying the moment and all the attention as she moved around the stage. Time seemed to stop as I watched her jump in the air, land and wiggle on her feet. As she made her way toward center stage, she spied me and smiled. I smiled back, and my head spun as I tried to make sense of what I was seeing. Then, as though in slow motion, I saw her jump and land on her left foot, which just buckled under her. She fell to the floor. My hand shot up to catch a gasp. She didn't get back up. I held my breath and waited a second. But Kate didn't move.

There was a great hush as Kate lay completely still, her hands covering her face. The backing track kept playing. I rushed forward and climbed on stage. The announcer and I reached her at the same time. Kate whimpered, her foot hanging kind of loose. It didn't look good. I felt like getting sick. Kate looked at me, crying gently.

"My foot, it fell off, didn't it?"

I crawled up to her face, not wanting her to see what had happened, and soon other kids came to see if she was OK. A paramedic arrived in double time and told Kate not to worry, his face gray. He spoke mechanically on his cell. Soon more first-aiders were there to help. I stayed close to Kate, trying to keep her calm, wanting to tell her everything would be OK. But all that came were floods of tears.

Chapter 30

What happened next was just a blur of frantic activity. Parents appeared to usher their kids away. I lay flat on my stomach, facing Kate, talking gently, sometimes saying nothing, just hushing her. The paramedic asked me repeatedly where our mom was, but I couldn't answer.

It was a terrible adventure, the dream turned real-life nightmare. Only when Kate tried to lift herself up did the screaming start, like the wail of a cat that had fallen down a well. I don't know how they got her onto the stretcher with all the crying and thrashing. It was horrendous to watch.

An ambulance rushed us through traffic straight to the ER. Kate had broken a bone in her foot, and whatever way she managed it, they felt they needed to operate, but were unable to because I wasn't her legal guardian. Instead, they gave her medication for the pain and tried to make her comfortable. I sat in a waiting area, shivering, unable to function. I just remember the hospital waiting area, fluorescent lights, a nurse asking me questions. I stared and answered as best as I could.

Later a doctor came, stethoscope around his neck. He shone a light into my eyes and said some words. Mrs. Gallagher and Martin's mom talked with him briefly. Mrs. Gallagher explained that she had to go back to the Union Centre and bring the other dancers back to Lakewood, and Martin's mom said they had to leave so that Declan could catch his flight.

The doctor gave me water and a pill for my headache, and I stretched myself across a couple of seats and stared at the different shoes that walked by. I found it funny. I found it funny that although I had stopped shivering, someone came and placed a blanket over me. Eventually, I fell asleep.

I woke later, completely confused. It was bright outside. I remembered that a doctor had tried to wake me in the middle of the night and tell me something. The clock said 6 a.m. A Hispanic receptionist came over when I wobbled to a stand. Before I got a chance to panic, she sat me down and spoke gently to me. She handed me an envelope, and I tore it open.

"Kate is doing OK. We can't do much until we get in touch with your parents. If you can get in contact with them, inform the attending immediately. Dr. Cross."

I knew they would have lots of trouble getting a hold of Old Buck. I asked the lady where the nearest pay phone was and looked at a scrunched-up ten. I asked if she had any quarters.

"My, you have a darling accent," she said, smiling. She took me behind the counter, picked up the phone and pressed zero. "Here you go, young lady."

I thanked her and dialed. It took ages, but eventually, Bailey answered.

"Jesus, Alex, I've been worried sick. Mrs. Gallagher called. What's happening now?"

"Kate fell. I don't know how — it just happened."

"Is she OK?"

"I think so. Where are your parents? Do they know?"

"Dad was back when I wasn't here. I called the hospital and left a message, but he still hasn't called."

"God, I don't even know where we are." I turned and looked blankly at the nurse.

"Cincinnati Children's hospital."

"You hear that? Have him call the emergency department when he gets back."

I set the phone down. I felt so sad and lonely, and I just wanted someone to talk to, someone who cared. Kate and I were both parentless and so far from home, and it was scary. I asked the receptionist if I could make one more call. She nodded, and I dialed. A sleepy voice answered.

"Hello? Hello, who is this?" But I couldn't speak. "Hello? Hello? Is there anyone there?"

"I'm sorry I called so early."

"Is that you, Alexandra?"

"Yes, Dr. Wallace. I'm sorry for calling you so early in the morning like this."

"That's OK." He yawned. "Tell me. Please tell me," he said, a little more awake. "Did Kate win?"

"You won't believe it. She won, Dr. Wallace."

"Well, that's just unbelievable," he said, sounding genuinely excited.

"But Dr. Wallace ..." And then I started to cry. "I reckon she's hurt real bad. We're in the hospital. I'm with the nurse."

I couldn't speak anymore. I handed the phone to the nurse. She spoke with him for a bit as I cried into my sweater, and then she connected him to another unit. She replaced the receiver and tried to console me.

"There, there, girl. She's in good hands."

She walked me to a cafeteria, ordered some breakfast and urged me to eat. She said she would come back shortly. Within five minutes — I had barely eaten two mouthfuls of cornflakes — a man in a green jacket came and told me to follow him. Kate lay in the back of an ambulance, asleep. I ran to her, calling her name, but she didn't wake up, not even when I held her hand. The paramedic told me to sit and relax, that she had been given something for the pain. Dr. Wallace knew the head of the hospital and had organized for us to get transferred back to Cleveland, to the hospital where Tammy was, so we could all be together. I couldn't believe such a saintly man existed. We left shortly after, and I didn't stir until we reached Cleveland.

Chapter 31

Old Buck was waiting for us outside the ER as the ambulance pulled up. His eyes were all red and puffy from tiredness, or maybe tears. As soon as the doctors had his consent, they brought Kate into the operating room. Buck drove me home—a silent trip—and I spent the rest of the day in my bedroom.

The following morning, Old Buck picked up Bailey and me and brought us to visit Kate. Tammy was allowed to hobble up from her ward. Kate's great cup sat on the table by her bed. Seemingly, her little buddy Martin and his mom had come to visit as she slept. She stared in awe, her poor face yellow after the operation. She was so brave.

"Can you believe it, Mom? I actually won," she said, enthusiastic despite the fatigue.

Tammy was still recovering from some sort of procedure. She winced as she attempted a smile.

The doctors didn't let us stay very long, because Kate's foot began to hurt. She needed more medication and rest. Bailey walked Tammy to her room. Old Buck asked me to help him bring back some tea and cookies from the cafeteria. Midway to the cafeteria, he stopped in the corridor and faced me.

"Alexandra, well, I don't know … you're just something. I don't know if you're good luck or bad. Both Tammy and I are outraged you pulled a stunt like that, taking our baby to another city. You're only fourteen, for Chrissake! And getting Bailey involved? As if she wasn't bad enough."

I swallowed. He wasn't done.

"It was stupid of you. How could you have risked our baby's safety, especially after all Tammy's gone through, what we've all gone through? So irresponsible!" He clenched his teeth.

I blubbered a bit, wanting to defend myself, but deciding against it. I didn't once take my eyes away from his gaze. His voice was firm, a little frightening, but he spoke fairly. And his eyes were just something. So big. But then they kind of changed, narrowed.

"That said, we are both amazed you did something so courageous out of the goodness of your heart for Kate. We know things have been hard, real hard, but you have been an inspiration to Kate. She loves you. You helped her achieve something she's dreamt of since she was very little."

"But look what happened. Look at what I did," I said, gesturing to the sterile white corridors, feeling sick to my stomach.

"An accident, sweetheart. That could happen in the garage, in the dancehall, at school, to anyone. You can't blame yourself for that."

I eventually gave a slow nod. I thought he was finished, but he kept staring at me.

"What?"

"There's one more piece of news I have for you."

My eyes opened in alarm.

"What is it?"

"Well, I guess, it's about your family. Things have come together pretty quick over the last week. We didn't want to get your hopes up, but looks as though everything is ready to go. You can go home, Alex, back to your family."

I couldn't believe what he was saying. I just shook my head in disbelief and punched him in the arm a couple times. Ecstasy seeped through my bloodstream, and I started jumping up and down and hollering, overjoyed. I was going back to my hometown, escaping the horridness of suburbia, back to my house, my dog, my Lucas, Mom and Dad, Vinnie, Grandpa. Old Buck's eyes were slanted.

"We'll miss you, though," he said. He grabbed me and bear-hugged the hell out of me. I squeezed back.

"When?"

"In the next few days. I'll take you as soon as Tammy is a little better."

We brought the tea for everyone, although I was only there in body; my spirit floated home to Kentucky.

Chapter 32

First thing I did when I got back to the house was call Vinnie and tell him the good news. He almost flipped. I spent the next two days thinking about all the things I wanted to do when got home. Breaking the news to Kate was going to be the hardest, and in the end, I decided to write her a letter. With us leaving in the early morning, it suited me to sneak out, and I must admit I did so without tears. I couldn't look at her as I placed the envelope on her bedside table and crept out of the room. I snuck into Tammy's room and hugged her.

"Thank you, Tammy, and I'm sorry. For everything."

"Be well, Alexandra," she said, and closed her eyes.

Only when the truck pulled out of the drive did the tears come.

It took us almost seven hours to get back to my hometown in Kentucky. It was so weird to see it all — the crummy old school, the convenience store, the people. Everybody had beards.

"Hey, old man, check out all the facials. You sure you don't want to stay here awhile? It's your kinda place."

Buck laughed his gruff old laugh. "I'm good, thanks."

I stopped smiling and looked across at him. I looked at him properly for maybe the first time ever, his reddish-brown hair, scraggly on top, his kind, yellow-green eyes. He looked back. "What? What you staring at, kid?"

"Nothin'," I said. "Hey, Old Buck, just how old are you anyway?"

"Coming up thirty-nine."

"Jeez, that's old! I hope I never get that old."

He smiled with his eyes and patted my leg.

"You know, Alex, you can come back for a visit any time you like. We'll always be here for you."

I just smiled.

We drove up the winding mountain road until we reached the green pastures on top. My little house was right there, near the birch in the center of the field. The sun chose that moment to peep out from behind some clouds. The smell of spring—grass and vanilla—overwhelmed my senses. My heart soared. I was home.

Harper, my trusted dog, was chasing a butterfly, Lucas not far behind him. My beautiful little Lucas. How his hair had grown. It was even more golden than mine. The truck had barely stopped, and I was bounding across the grass. Lucas's face was blank. I don't think he recognized me at first. Then he opened his arms and ran to meet me. We threw our arms around each other, and I kissed and kissed the top of his head and his cheeks.

"Boy, Alex, I thought you was never coming back. Your hair looks funny." Then he just broke his face laughing.

Mom and Dad came to see what the commotion was, and we all hugged like a great big happy family. Dad commented on my accent, and I almost had to try to make sure I sounded Kentuckian again.

Everyone looked so healthy and well. Mom had her hair done, and her cheeks had a fresh shine. It was only the kitchen and part of the living room that had been damaged. We had a new stove, countertop and kitchen table, and the front door was brand new too. Everything looked good, except the Christmas tree was still up in the corner of the living room. It was old and brown and didn't smell like the holidays anymore.

Old Buck didn't stay long, just had a quick cup of coffee. I guess he was anxious to get back to Lakewood and tend to the two ailing members of his family. Mom had just been to the store, and she made me franks and beans. It used to be my favorite. Strangely, I didn't like it much anymore, but I ate it anyway, out of politeness.

For the rest of the day, Lucas and I just played games, went fishing, rode the horse, and it felt awesome to be able to run around in just a T-shirt again, although it still wasn't warm enough for shorts.

After dinner, I sat on Dad's knee, and Lucas sat at his feet. Dad told us a story about when he had been in the Middle East, at war. That night, I got tired early. Before I went to sleep, I fished the old music box out of my closet. I wiped the dust off and opened the lid. Lucas came and sat beside me, and we watched the blonde figurine twirl to the chimes without saying anything. Finally, Lucas looked at me with his big, bright eyes.

"Geez, Alex, that little girl — she looks just like you." I grimaced, then clenched my teeth as I watched him get under the covers of his bed. I stared at the blonde figurine with the dead eyes, crooked nose and melted face, lipstick trying its best to disguise. Then I got into bed and sighed. It felt weird to be home, but good. My heart was content.

* * *

I spent the following day playing with Lucas. When we got tired, we lay on the grass and threw the ball for Harper, who ran after it and didn't come back. The sun bounced off our faces while we watched funny-shaped clouds sail across the sky. Lucas couldn't stop talking, just like Kate. It must have been a genetic condition that I escaped.

"Look at that one. It looks like a pig," he said. "And look at that one. It's either a goat or a polar bear. That one's a giant spider." He snuggled his head against my shoulder.

"Do you know how clouds are formed, Lucas?"

He shot up quick. Mom had cut his hair again. His face was so naughty looking, but I knew he really wasn't.

"It's when you stretch your hands out as far as you can go," he replied confidently, demonstrating. I got up onto my elbows and spat a piece of grass out of my mouth.

"Noooo. Where did that come from?"

His face got serious. "What does 'clouds formed' mean?"

"Clouds formed means how clouds are made."

"Umm, cotton wool?"

I laughed and ruffled his hair. "C'mon, silly. Let's go fix that old radio," I said, getting up.

Lucas followed, more obedient than Harper. "Hey, Alex, you know how mustard is formed?"

He had found an old radio when he was out "hunting" and stored it for "safe-keeping" in our room. It wasn't hard to fix, just needed a new plug. We turned the dial to find some music and ended up with some old country and western station. A song played that sounded just like Irish dance music. I made some space in the room and did some Irish dance moves. Lucas laughed, but by the end of the music I had him holding my hand as I showed him the over-two-threes that Kate had shown me. I missed Kate a little and wished I could have her here with me too. I also kind of missed the dancing. Maybe during summer I would start up ballet again, I thought.

I wanted to know how Kate was doing, so I called Lakewood, and Tammy answered. She told me Kate had been crying since she read my letter, and wouldn't leave her room. She didn't want to talk to me on the phone. That just crushed me. It was hard enough to understand everything that had happened, never mind make others see.

Later that day, I met up with Vinnie. He looked so different. He stood taller, and his biceps were tearing up his T-shirt. I told him I was so happy to be back. He told me that he loved me and hoped I'd never leave. We sat and talked and kissed under a sugar maple all afternoon.

The next few days, I just relaxed. I was going to start back in school after the weekend. Friday night, Mom and Dad had a friend around, and after dinner, we were sent to bed kinda early while they had some beers and listened to music.

* * *

There was a horrible cry that woke me gasping from my sleep. I thought I was having a nightmare, but I was wrong. Another yell soon followed. They were arguing. Lucas didn't wake until the first bottle shattered. He got up and saw me shivering in the bed.

"Alex?" he said softly. He came into my bed, and I held him a moment. The shouting continued. I went to the doorway and opened it quietly. The yelling and crying came rushing in. I listened in the hall, the horror returning, the remission short-lived. I eyed the two through a crack in the living room door.

That's when I saw Momma slap Dad real hard across the face. He just stared back, speechless. She kept shouting and shoving Dad. Lucas was crying in the bedroom. I felt sick, and I wanted to scream, but couldn't. I wanted to fight, wanted to intervene, but nothing would help; I knew that.

"Deborah, I can't do this. You're out of your mind!"

The words cut me. Mom was out of control, pushing Dad in the chest. They were both so drunk. Another bottle smashed, and still they ignored the cries from the bedroom, Lucas frightened for his poor little life. I went to him, held him in his bed, a cold clammy sweat on the little man's brow. Time passed so slow. I hoped that soon I would wake up and home would be like I remembered it. But really, it was like I remembered it, if I was being honest with myself.

Eventually, Lucas stopped shaking, just whimpered. I shushed him as best I could. The screaming stopped, the house was quiet, and no matter how much I reassured Lucas, my own fears remained. He eventually fell asleep. I ventured out to the kitchen, some blood and broken glass to skip by on my way to the telephone. Even though I was terrified, I knew that my life would only be miserable if I allowed it to be. I knew different now. I knew it didn't have to be this way. Kate's courageous dance face flickered in my mind's eye.

It was almost 3 a.m., and as bad as I felt, I knew I had to do it. Tapping the digits quietly, I waited for a voice to answer.

"Hello? It's Alex."

"Is everything all right, honey?"

"John, it's happening again."

About the author

Seán de Gallai first took an interest in writing in 2007 after taking a scriptwriting course. In 2011 he attended the Faber Academy in Dublin. His first book effort, *Addicted to Candy*, about a boy who was addicted to candy, was a resounding failure. His second effort, *The Hard Way*, about a bunch of idiotic teenagers who refused to do things the easy way, died a tragic death. *The Dancer. Steps from the Dark* is his third-time lucky. Seán is a primary school teacher and works in Dublin.

www.seandegallai.com
seandegallai@gmail.com

Printed in Great
Britain
by Amazon